Praise For Sandra Brown

>⊷⊷○⊶⊷◄

"Millions of readers clamor for the compelling contemporary novels of Sandra Brown. And no wonder! She fires your imagination with irresistible characters, unexpected plot twists, scandalous secrets, and sexual tension so electric you *feel* the zing."
—*The Literary Guild* **magazine**

"Author Sandra Brown proves herself top-notch."
—*Associated Press*

"One of our times' most talented authors of women's fiction."
—*Affaire de Coeur*

>⊷⊷○⊶⊷◄

SANDRA BROWN

ELOQUENT SILENCE

WARNER
VISION
BOOKS

A Time Warner Company

WARNER BOOKS EDITION

Copyright © 1982 by Sandra Brown
All rights reserved.

Cover design by Jackie Merri Meyer
Cover photograph by Herman Estevez
Hand lettering by Carl Dellacroce

This Warner Books Edition is published by arrangement with the author.

Warner Vision is a trademark of Warner Books, Inc.

Warner Books, Inc.
1271 Avenue of the Americas
New York, NY 10020

W A Time Warner Company

Printed in the United States of America
First Warner Books Printing: January, 1995

10 9 8 7 6 5 4 3

TO MY PARENTS.
Thank you for loving me.

Dear Reader,

For years before I began writing general fiction, I wrote genre romances under several pseudonyms. *Eloquent Silence* was originally published more than ten years ago (under my first pen name, Rachel Ryan.)

This story reflects the trends and attitudes that were popular at that time, but its themes are eternal and universal. As in all romance fiction, the plot revolves around star-crossed lovers. There are moments of passion, anguish, and tenderness—all integral facets of falling in love.

I very much enjoyed writing romances. They're optimistic in orientation and have a charm unique to any other form of fiction. If this is your first taste of it, please enjoy.

Sandra Brown

Chapter One

"**D**o you think your husband knows about us, darling?" The man brushed his lips across the woman's forehead as he clasped her in a desperate embrace.

"Even if he does, I don't care," she declared. "I'm tired of hiding. I want to proclaim our love to everyone."

"Oh, my love, my love." The man lowered his head. His nose bumped into the woman's in a most unromantic way.

"*Cut!*"

Lauri Parrish jumped when the exasperated command thundered from the loudspeaker in a voice that reverberated like God's from Mount Sinai.

"What in the hell is going on today? Can't you two get anything right? We've been on this same damn scene for an hour and a half." A brief silence hung in the air while the actors and crew shifted uncomfortably. "I'm coming down."

Lauri watched in fascination as the actress turned to her leading man and said scathingly, "I was to lean into Camera One, Drake. Not you."

"Then you'd better learn to count, Lois. That was Camera Three. Besides, aren't you afraid Camera One will detect your facelift scars?"

"Bastard," hissed the actress as she shoved past the amused cameramen and tapped across the concrete floor of the television studio in the direction of the dressing rooms.

The whole episode intrigued Lauri Parrish, who had surprisingly found herself on the set of *The Heart's Answer*, a popular daytime soap opera. She never watched television during the day, for she was always working, but everyone in America knew about this particular program. Many working women planned their lunch hours around the drama's telecast in order to keep up with the sexual exploits and personal crises of Dr. Glen Hambrick.

A few days before, Dr. Martha Norwood, founder of the Norwood Institute for the Deaf where Lauri was a teacher, had approached her with an offer.

"We have a student here, Jennifer Rivington, whose father is thinking of taking her out of the school."

"I know who Jennifer is," Lauri said. "She's only partially impaired, but she's totally uncommunicative."

"For that reason her father is very concerned."

"Father? No mother?"

Dr. Norwood hesitated a moment before she said, "No, her mother is deceased. Her father has an unusual job. It has been necessary for him to board Jennifer with us since she was an infant. She hasn't adjusted well. Now he wants to hire a private tutor to stay with her at home. I thought you might be interested, Lauri."

Lauri knit her auburn brows together in a soft frown. "I don't know. Could you be more specific?"

The gray-haired lady with the intelligent blue eyes studied her most dedicated teacher. "Not just now. I will tell you that Mr. Rivington wants the tutor to take Jennifer to New Mexico to live. He has a house in a small community in the mountains." Dr. Norwood smiled gently. "I know you'd like to get away from New York. And you're certainly qualified to take on a job like this."

Lauri laughed softly. "Having grown up in Nebraska, I find New York somewhat stifling and crowded. I've been here eight years, and I still miss the wide open spaces." She brushed back a vagrant auburn curl. "It sounds to me as if Mr. Rivington is shirking his responsibility to rear his own daughter. Is he one of those parents who resents the child for being deaf?"

Dr. Norwood looked down at her well-manicured hands, which were clasped together on top of her desk. "Don't be so quick to judge, Lauri," she chided gently. Sometimes her protégée let her temper get the best of her. If Lauri Parrish had a fault, it was jumping to conclusions. "As I mentioned, the circumstances are unusual."

She stood up briskly, indicating that the meeting was over. "You don't have to make a decision today, Lauri. I want you to observe Jennifer for the next few days. Spend some time with her. Then, when it's convenient, I think you and Mr. Rivington should get together and talk."

"I'll cooperate any way I can, Doctor Norwood."

When Lauri reached the frosted-glass door, Dr. Norwood halted her. "Lauri, in case you were wondering, money is no object."

Lauri answered with complete honesty. "Doctor Norwood, if I accepted any private tutoring job, it would be because I thought that is what the child needed."

"I thought so," Dr. Norwood replied, smiling.

This morning Dr. Norwood had slipped her a piece of paper with an address on it and said, "You are to go to this address at three o'clock today. Ask for Mr. D. L. Rivington. He'll be expecting you."

Lauri had been astonished when the cab driver stopped at the specified address and she saw that it was a building that housed studios for a television network. She had entered the building with her curiosity in the mysterious Mr. Rivington piqued. When she asked for him at the reception desk, the beautiful young receptionist looked puzzled for a moment then giggled as she said, "Third floor."

Lauri started for the elevator but the girl said, "Just a minute. What's your name?" Lauri gave it. The receptionist ran her finger down a typed list, then said, "There you are. Miss L. Parrish. You can go right up, but be very quiet. They're still taping."

Lauri stepped off the elevator and found herself in a cavernous television studio. She was awed by the equipment and activity.

The barnlike studio was sectioned off into the various sets for the soap opera. One set was furnished with a hospital bed and dummy medical equipment. Another was a living room. There was a tiny kitchen set barely four feet across. She wandered around the studio, peeking curiously at the sets, trying not to trip on the miles of cable that snaked over the floor and coiled around the studio cameras and monitors.

"Hey, cutie, whaddaya need?" a jean-clad cameraman asked her in a fresh chirp.

Startled, Lauri stammered, "I—uh—yes. Mr. Rivington? I need to see him."

"Mr. Rivington?" the cameraman crowed as if she had said something funny. "That's heavy. Did you pass muster downstairs?" She nodded. "Then you can see him. Can you wait till we get this scene in the can?"

"I—yes," she said, agreeing to whatever his jargon was supposed to mean.

"Stand over here and be quiet and don't touch anything," the technician warned.

5

Sandra Brown

Lauri stood behind the cameras that were focused on a set of what looked to her like a hospital lounge.

Now, during this unexpected break, she watched the actor who was the heartthrob of millions of American women. He was sitting leisurely on one of the prop tables, eating an apple he had pilfered from the basket on the table. Lauri wondered if his fans would be so enthralled with him if they had heard Drake Sloan speak so unchivalrously to his co-star. But then, that rudeness was part of his appeal, wasn't it? He was the macho male doctor who ran roughshod over everyone else in the fictitious hospital and reduced all the women to quivering jelly with his domineering manner and seductive good looks.

Well, thought Lauri objectively, *that* many women couldn't all be wrong. He did have a certain animal appeal—if you liked that type. It was his coloring that first attracted one's attention. His hair was an unusual ash-brown, but under the studio lights it appeared almost silver. Contrasting with that strange silver hair were dark, thick brows and a dark mustache. The mustache added to the insolent sensuality of his bottom lip and drove housewives, career girls, and grandmothers wild with desire. His most arresting feature was his eyes. They were a vibrant green. In close-up shots, they smoldered with a fire guaranteed to melt the heart of the most frigid female.

From her observation point outside the circle formed by the intense studio lights, Lauri watched Drake Sloan

6

as he stood up, stretched like a lazy cat, and tossed the apple core into a wastebasket with an expert hook shot.

Lauri scoffed at his costume. She doubted that any doctor wearing pants that tight could go about the business of healing the sick. The green surgical attire had been tailored to fit Drake Sloan's tall, lean frame like a second skin. The shirt was cut in a deep V that revealed a chest furred with dark hair. As if that would be allowed in an operating room! Lauri thought.

Hearing a soothing voice behind her, Lauri turned. The man she assumed to be the one who had spoken from the control room above was coming toward the set with the offended actress under his solicitous arm.

"He won't take direction," she was complaining. "He knows the blocking, but when the camera comes on, he does whatever he damn well pleases."

"I know, I know, Lois. Can't you be my dependable girl and tolerate him for me?" the director asked commiseratively. "Let's get through today's schedule, and then we'll talk about it over a drink. I'll speak to Drake. Okay? Now, let me see that dazzling smile."

What rubbish. Lauri groaned silently. Artistic temperament. She knew all about it. Tell them what they want to hear and alleviate the paranoia until the next outbreak.

The two joined Drake Sloan on the set, and the three of them held a brief discussion. The crew, who had been enjoying the respite by smoking cigarettes, reading magazines, or talking together, resumed their positions behind the cameras and adjusted the connecting ear-

7

phones onto their heads. It was through these that each one received his instructions from the director in the control booth.

The boom-microphone operator was toying with his intricate machine. With its erratic, disjointed movements, it resembled the skeleton of some prehistoric animal.

The director kissed Lois on the cheek and stepped back off the set. "Before I go back upstairs, let's walk through the scene one more time. Kiss her like you mean it, Drake. She's your lover, remember?"

"Has your lover ever had anchovy pizza for lunch, Murray?"

Lois screamed in indignation.

The crew burst out laughing at her expense. Murray managed to calm her down once again. Then he said, "Tape's rolling."

One of the cameras had assumed a new position that blocked Lauri's vantage point. In spite of herself she had grown interested in this videotaping session. She moved to an unobstructed spot where she could see and hear clearly. This time when their trite dialogue was completed, Drake Sloan took Lois in his arms and kissed her fiercely.

Lauri's heart skipped a beat as she watched his lips close over the actress's. One could almost feel that kiss, could almost imagine ... She leaned against the prop table to get a better view. The sound of shattering glass swept everyone's eyes away from the actors on the set. They were all staring at her!

She jumped in reaction, mortified that she had called attention to herself. She hadn't seen the tall glass vase on the table. Now it lay splintered in a thousand pieces on the studio floor.

"Dammit!" Drake Sloan shouted. "What now?" He pushed Lois away from him and crossed the studio floor in three long determined strides. Murray followed him, dispirited and vexed, but calm. The actor bore down on Lauri and she cowered under his anger.

"Who the hell—"

"She's here to see Mr. Rivington," interrupted the cheeky cameraman who had spoken to Lauri before.

Drake Sloan pinned her to the floor with his green eyes, which were now glinting under the dark brows. They opened wider in curiosity. "Mr. Rivington, huh?" There was a twitter of laughter from the crew. "Murray, I had no idea you'd started allowing the Girl Scouts to visit the set for their field trips." This time the crew laughed in earnest.

Lauri was unimpressed by Drake Sloan's comic abilities and furious that she had become the object of his derision. Her temper matched the red highlights in her hair, and her brown eyes narrowed on him as she felt her hackles rise.

"I'm sorry I interrupted your—thing," she said haughtily. She didn't know what to call the taping session and didn't care. She turned away from Drake Sloan's cynical stare and spoke to Murray who seemed to be a decent person. "I'm Lauri Parrish and I was told to meet Mr. Rivington here at three o'clock. I apologize for the delay I've caused."

"It's just one of many today, I'm afraid," he said, sighing heavily. Glancing furtively at Drake Sloan, he said, "Mr. Rivington is busy. Could you wait for him in my office? He should be able to join you shortly."

"Yes, thank you," she answered. "I'll pay for the vase."

"Forget it. Go up the stairs and through the control room. It's the office right across the hall."

"Thank you," Lauri repeated before she turned and, aware that every eye in the studio was on her, climbed the circular staircase. By the time she reached the top, Murray had everyone back in position.

She would have liked to stop and look at the control board—an intimidating, complicated computer. The various monitors suspended above it allowed the director to see what shots the cameras had, and she saw Drake Sloan's face rolling into and out of focus. She was tempted to stick her tongue out at him.

She collapsed in the only available chair in the office besides the one of cracked vinyl that stood behind the cluttered desk. She studied the dusty pictures on the wall that had captured Murray what's-his-name in the company of actresses, directors, and VIPs.

Who was this Mr. Rivington anyway? Was he a network executive? A technician? No. He was someone who had money, for the Norwood Institute was expensive. And Mr. Rivington boarded Jennifer there, which increased the expense threefold. The minutes seemed to stretch out, and Lauri was beginning to grow impatient when she heard the door open behind her.

Drake Sloan walked in and shut the door quietly behind him.

Lauri stood up in a defensive motion. "I'm to meet—"

"I'm D. L. Rivington, Jennifer's father."

Lauri felt her lips forming a small round O. She stared at him as he leaned against the door. He had changed clothes. He was wearing jeans and a pullover sweater. The loose sleeves had been casually pushed up to his elbows.

"You seem surprised."

She nodded.

"Doctor Norwood didn't tell you my professional name." It wasn't a question. He scratched his ear absently. "No, I guess she wouldn't. No doubt she was afraid of prejudicing you against me. Actors have abominable reputations, you know." The corners of his mouth lifted in the semblance of a grin that vanished as quickly as it appeared. "Especially if everything you read in the fan magazines is true. Did you know that I forced my current girlfriend to have an abortion last week? At least that's what I read," he said caustically.

Lauri was still too shocked to speak. She thought wryly about the other teachers in the school and what they would say if they knew she was in the same room with Dr. Glen Hambrick/Drake Sloan.

Lauri was always cool and competent—except when her temper gained control. Why, then, was she standing here with her sweaty hands clasped together? She hadn't moved since he had announced his identity. Her tongue felt glued to the roof of her mouth.

"If it gives you any comfort, Miss Parrish, you're not quite what I expected either." He pushed away from the door and instinctively Lauri took a step backward.

He smiled the smile that deepened the famous dimple in his right cheek. He knew she was uneasy at being alone with him in the small office. That infuriated her: Who was he anyway? She wasn't going to stand here like a groupie in the presence of some rock-star idol and stutter like an idiot. Drake Sloan put his pants on one leg at a time just like everyone else.

"It's *Ms.* Parrish."

He lifted an amused eyebrow and muttered, "I should have known." His superior attitude irritated her.

She said in her most professional voice, "Doctor Norwood sent me here to talk about Jennifer, Mr. Rivington."

"Drake. Would you like some coffee?" He indicated a coffee maker on which a pot of coffee as black and thick as pitch was warming. Lauri didn't want any, but realized it would give her something to hold except her other hand.

"Yes, please."

He crossed to the small table and looked dubiously into a cup whose degree of cleanliness was questionable. He poured the coffee and raised an inquiring brow. "Cream? Sugar?"

"Cream."

He added a powdered product to the coffee and stirred it with a stained plastic spoon that had obviously already been used for that purpose. He handed her the cup. She closed her hand around it. He didn't release it at first, but continued to hold the cup until she looked up at him. She swallowed hard at her first glimpse into the emerald eyes that now reflected an image of her.

"I've never seen anyone with eyes the same color as their hair," he said.

Lauri knew her auburn hair was beautiful. It was a deep russet that lightened in the sunlight. What made her more than an exceptional redhead was the color of her eyes. They were such a light brown, they looked almost topaz until one compared them to her hair, when they took on that unusual auburn hue. The yellow linen suit accented her hair and eyes and added a glow to her honey-apricot complexion.

Thank you wouldn't really be an appropriate response to his statement, for it hadn't been a true compliment. Lauri only smiled tremulously and tried more forcefully to pull the coffee cup out of his hand. He gave in and turned to pour himself one.

"Tell me about my daughter, *Ms.* Parrish," he said, stressing the form of address with heavy sarcasm. He went behind the desk, settling into the creaking chair, and propped his feet on the desk.

Lauri sat tense and straight on the chair facing him. She sipped her coffee. It was as bad as she had anticipated it would be. He chuckled at her grimace. "I apologize for the quality."

"It's fine, Mr. Sl—Rivington."

She was staring down into the coffee cup and, when he didn't say anything, she looked up at him. To her surprise he signed his name with the alphabet for the deaf. *D-R-A-K-E*. His dark brows lowered over his eyes, which seemed to insist she use his first name.

She licked her lips nervously, smiled slightly, and then signed *Lauri*. He lowered his feet, leaned forward in the chair, rested his elbows on the desk, and supported his chin on his fists.

Lauri decided now was as good a time as any to test his expertise at sign language. Dr. Norwood had been judiciously reticent about Drake Rivington. Lauri now understood that her supervisor had wanted her to form her own opinion of him. Using slow and precise gestures, Lauri asked him in sign language, *Do you use sign language with Jennifer?*

"I understood *Jennifer*, that's all," he said when she stopped.

She tried again and asked him in sign, *How old is your daughter?* He didn't react at all. He just sat there staring at her with those green eyes that had suddenly become expressionless. Lauri signed *What color is her hair*? Nothing. *Do you love Jennifer*?

"*Jennifer* again. I'm sorry I don't know the rest. I think this is *love*." He crossed his arms over his chest as she had done.

"Yes, that's right, Drake. From now on, this will be your name so you won't have to spell it out each time."

She made the sign for the letter *D* and touched it to the middle of her forehead. "This is *father*," she said, touching her forehead with her thumb, her other fingers spread. "We'll combine the two. See?"

He nodded. "This is *Lauri*." She made the letter *L* and stroked the side of her face from cheekbone to chin. "This is *girl*," she said, stroking her cheek with her thumb while her hand was held in a gentle fist. "See how we combine the two signs to form someone's name?"

"Yeah," he said with a trace of excitement. "For *Jennifer* we make the letter *J* with our little finger and then a curly sign to indicate her curly hair."

"Exactly!" They smiled across at each other, and for a moment their eyes locked. There was a strange but pleasant stirring deep within her. She had a fleeting knowledge of how other women must feel when they watched this handsome face on their television screens each afternoon. He was indeed charismatic and he knew it. If she didn't watch herself, he could deter her from the things she had come to say to him.

"Drake," she was signing everything now, even as

she spoke it, in the habit of teachers who worked with the deaf. "Doctor Norwood asked me to evaluate Jennifer's progress. I've been observing her for several days. I feel that my opinion is an educated one, but that's all it is, an opinion. However, I'm going to be totally honest with you."

"I want you to be. I'm sure you think the worst of a father who has had his daughter institutionalized for most of her three years, but I love her. I'm concerned about her. And I want to do what's best for her." He stood up and went to the window. With his back to Lauri, he looked through the grimy glass.

"Please watch me sign, Drake. It will help you learn it." He faced her again as if about to issue a challenge, but he shrugged and returned to the chair.

She continued quietly. "You are fortunate that Jennifer is not profoundly deaf. I'm sure you know by now that her deafness is the sensory neural type that, at this point in time, is irreparable. She can hear some loud noises. For instance she can distinguish between a helicopter and a whistle." She paused to see if he would comment. He didn't, so she continued. "Unfortunately she doesn't know the name for a whistle or a helicopter. Or maybe she knows and just doesn't reveal to us that she does. She's almost totally unresponsive to any communication."

The lines on either side of his mouth tightened. "Are you telling me she's retarded?"

"No, not at all," Lauri emphasized. "She's exceptionally bright. It's my opinion that she lacks in— Some children need to be taught on a one-to-one basis. I personally feel that it has been detrimental to Jennifer's development for her to be institutionalized. She needs to be in a home environment where she is constantly in the company of someone who . . . who . . ." she trailed off, not wanting to say what she thought might offend him.

"Who *loves* her? Is that what you're stammering about? I told you I love her. I didn't lock her up in that school because I was ashamed of her."

"I didn't mean to—"

"Of course you did!" he barked. "Since you're so smart, you tell me what a widower with an infant child does with that child. Especially if that child is deaf. Huh? That fancy school of yours is expensive, you know. I have to work hard to afford it. And the medical bills after a million tests that don't tell you one damn thing except that your little girl is deaf, which you already knew, or you wouldn't have put her through those awful goddamn tests in the first place."

He paused to draw a breath, his green eyes flashing dangerously. "At least we concur on one thing. Jennifer needs to be privately tutored." He stood up abruptly, sending the chair flying backward on squeaky coasters. "But not by you." He stormed around the desk and braced his strong arms on the sides of her chair, imprisoning her in it.

"I told Doctor Norwood I wanted someone responsible. I was looking for a grandmotherly type in a baggy sweater with large pockets—not a chick in a designer suit." His eyes flicked over her body in an insulting assessment. "Someone with gray hair pulled back into a neat bun, not flaming red hair flowing in the unmistakable lines of a Sassoon cut. Someone slightly overweight with a plump, matronly figure, not flaunting pert little breasts and a tight little rear." Lauri flushed hotly with anger and embarrassment. How dare he!

"Jennifer's tutor should have thick ankles and wear sensible shoes, not—" He indicated her trim calves, encased in sheer stockings and the high-heeled ankle-strap sandals she was wearing. "You don't look like a tutor for a deaf child. You look like one of the girls who hand out the fragrance samples in Bergdorf's."

He leaned down even closer until his head was almost touching hers. Before she could react, he buried his face in the soft hair behind her ear. "You smell like them too," he whispered huskily.

For an instant Lauri couldn't breathe. But when she could, his own scent assailed her. It was clean and musky and male. What was the matter with her? She jerked her head away from him.

"You— Let me up from here this instant," she demanded, pushing against the wall of his chest. Surprisingly he straightened up and stepped away from the chair as she bolted out of it. She took several deep, restorative breaths before she said, "I may not live up to your expectations, but you certainly confirmed mine, Mr. Sloan." She said the name like an epithet.

"You don't deserve your daughter. She's beautiful and intelligent and sweet. But she's dying. Do you hear me? She's dying emotionally because her only parent hasn't taken it upon himself to learn a language she can understand, much less try to teach her that language. It's parents like you who set deaf education back to the Helen Keller days. I'm a teacher—"

"You're a girl."

"I'm a woman—"

"Ahhh, now we get to my next point," he said, pointing an accusing finger at her. "Don't pretend you didn't like my touching you. I know better. How do I know that if I set you up out in New Mexico, you won't run off with the first unattached man that comes along? Isn't that what all you liberated career girls really want? A husband?"

Lauri could feel the heat of her fury burning to the roots of her hair. "I've had one. It wasn't a very happy marriage."

"You divorced?"

"He died."

"How convenient."

She whirled away from him before she could say anything else that might prove to be regrettable. After all, Dr. Norwood had sent her on this mission and would expect a report. At the door she turned to see him leaning against the desk with ankles crossed. His smug, satisfied attitude was evident in the mocking eyes, the indolent stance, and the curled lip under the thick mustache.

Slowly and deliberately Lauri said, "You are the most arrogant, ill-mannered, insufferable—" She signed the last word.

"What does that mean?" he snapped, as he quickly pushed away from the desk.

"You figure it out, Mr. Sloan."

She slammed the door behind her.

Chapter Two

❦

"Lauri, you'll never guess—"

"Brigette, I'm in the middle of a class. What is it?"

The teacher who had burst into Lauri's classroom of seven-year-old students looked completely flustered, and she stammered as she said, "You'll never guess who's out there asking for you. I mean, I've seen him a million times. I'd know him anywhere. But then there he was, standing out in the hallway, asking for you—"

"Slow down, Brigette, you're upsetting the children. They think something is wrong." Lauri knew whom her friend must be referring to, but she didn't want anyone to know that her heart had lurched at the thought of

21

seeing Drake Rivington again. To even the most discriminating eye she appeared cool and indifferent.

It had been over a week since their meeting at the television studio. When she returned from that inauspicious interview, Dr. Norwood asked her about it.

"I don't think I was quite what Mr. Rivington had in mind, though I think we agreed that Jennifer needs special care and training on a more personal level."

"Oh, I'm so disappointed, Lauri," the administrator said. "I just knew you two would hit it off and you could take Jennifer to New Mexico. Of course, I was dreading losing you."

Lauri smiled. "Well, you'll not be losing me for a while. I think you'd better have another recommendation in mind. Mr. Rivington will no doubt be calling you."

Lauri offered no more information, and Dr. Norwood didn't press her. The woman was uncannily perceptive. Did she guess that the meeting hadn't gone well?

All that week Lauri tried to put Drake Rivington out of her mind. She had spent so much time with Jennifer lately that she found it hard to stop those daily visits with the child. Jennifer was in a group of students younger than those Lauri taught, and she had been seeing Drake's daughter after regular classroom hours.

Jennifer was a beautiful child. She was well-behaved—almost too well-behaved, Lauri thought. Her hair was pale blond, and riotous curls tangled around her small head. Her eyes—exactly like her father's—were a deep green, fringed with contradictory dark lashes. She was delicate and dainty and never got dirty or did anything to provoke anyone's anger.

Lauri had prided herself on her objectivity, but the little girl with the big sad eyes was getting to her. It only took a few days for her to know that she wanted to become Jennifer's tutor. She wanted to take the child out of the orderly, well-furnished dormitory and put her in a cheerful, cluttered room.

Her thoughts along these lines would invariably return to Jennifer's father, and the bubble would burst. She could never work for such a man and live in his house. It didn't matter that he would be two thousand miles away. He had insulted her as a woman and as a professional. Besides, he didn't want her for Jennifer's tutor.

She would have denied to anyone that she had been watching *The Heart's Answer*. For the last few days, when it was time for the silly drama, she could be found in front of the television set in the teachers' lounge. Every time she saw Drake on the twelve-inch screen, disturbing things would happen to her. Her heartbeat escalated and her palms grew moist; a warm heaviness settled in the middle of her body and spread to her limbs, rendering them useless. She could vividly recall him leaning over her and nuzzling her hair. Small mannerisms she would never have noticed in anyone else characterized him in a frighteningly familiar way. That was crazy! She had spent no more than fifteen minutes with him. Yet, she felt she knew each nuance of his personality intimately.

Now Brigette had barged into her classroom, raving

about the actor's good looks and charm. What Brigette didn't know was that the man was unforgivably conceited, rude, and impertinent.

"Can you believe that Drake Sloan is Jennifer Rivington's father? I wondered why we never saw her parents. He comes here at night through Doctor Norwood's apartment for his visits with Jennifer. I guess he's afraid of being swarmed by fans like me." Brigette giggled. "And he's asking for you as if he knew you!"

"He does."

Brigette was silenced by this bit of information and stared at Lauri as if the young woman had sprouted wings. "You *know* him and you never said—"

"Brigette, what is it you want?"

"Wha-what is it I want?" she parroted. "I just told you, Doctor Glen Hambrick or Mr. Rivington or whatever you want to call him is waiting to see you."

"Tell him I'm busy."

"What!" Brigette shrieked, and for an instant Lauri wished she shared the handicap of her students. Sometimes deafness could be considered a blessing. "You don't mean that, Lauri. Are you insane? The sexiest man in the whole world is—"

"I think that's exaggerating, Brigette," Lauri said dryly. "I'm busy. If Mr. Rivington wants to see me, he'll have to wait until this class is over."

"I'd be happy to."

The deep, low voice projected into the room with the modulated tones of a professional actor. He was standing framed in the doorway, looking straight at Lauri. Her heart skipped a beat before returning to a steady, though accelerated, pace.

Brigette had lost her well-exercised capacity for speech and stood openmouthed as she stared at Drake. Not wanting to create a scene, the details of which Lauri was sure Brigette would broadcast to the entire faculty, she said softly, "Would you excuse us, Brigette? As Mr. Rivington has already interrupted my class, I suppose I must just as well see him." He only grinned at her sarcasm.

Brigette walked trancelike toward the door and stood in front of Drake like a mannequin until he moved aside and ushered her into the hall. His smile was devastating, and his mustache twitched in amusement over Brigette's hypnotic state.

How perfectly sickening, Lauri thought. What was it about this man that reduced intelligent women to somnambulant morons? He was an ordinary man. Well, perhaps a little more than ordinary looking, Lauri conceded when he turned back to face her.

"Hello, Ms. Parrish. I hope I'm not interrupting you."

"You are, and you're not sorry for it at all."

His grin deepened, and so did the dimple in his cheek. "You're right, I'm not. But I have Doctor Norwood's permission to be here. She thought I should observe your teaching techniques."

Her lips pursed in disapproval. Then she sighed. She'd give in this time, but she didn't have to do it gracefully.

"Children," she said, signing as she spoke, "this is Mr. Rivington. Do you all know Jennifer Rivington? This is her father."

The children acknowledged him with smiles and a few signed *hi*. Some of the more auditory children even spoke the word.

"Have a seat, Mr. Rivington." She indicated a low chair. He frowned at her as he eased his long frame into the ridiculously small chair. Some of the children laughed, and Lauri found it hard not to join them. When he was finally situated, his knees were almost touching his chin.

He was impeccably dressed in brown slacks and a camel blazer. His shirt was white, but striped with varying shades of brown. A dark brown necktie was knotted at his throat.

"We're working on prepositions, Mr. Rivington. Come here, Jeff, and show Jennifer's father what you've learned."

On the bulletin board Lauri had tacked several large, glossy pictures of apples. Bright yellow worms with happy smiles and big eyes were placed either on, under, behind, in or in front of the apples. The child learned the concept, the printed word, and the sign by positioning the worms on the apples.

"Now you do it," Lauri said, turning to Drake when all the students had gone through the exercise.

"What?" he cried.

The children started laughing when Lauri put her hand

under Drake's elbow and pulled him to his feet, standing him in front of the bulletin board. She pointed a yardstick to a particular apple and asked in sign, "Where is the worm?"

The green eyes bore into her as if he wanted to throttle her, but she only smiled sweetly. "Surely this is not too hard for you," she purred.

He gave her the sign for the correct preposition.

"In a complete sentence, please."

The long, brown fingers signed the complete sentence just as the dismissal bell rang. A few of the children could hear its shrill sound, and they began to shift restlessly in their chairs.

"Okay, class, go!" Lauri said as she signed it. They needed no encouragement to race toward the door, and she was left alone with Drake.

"That was a clever trick. Do you give each visiting parent that kind of personal attention?" he snarled.

"Most visiting parents have the good manners not to barge into the middle of a class and demand personal attention."

"Touché," he said without the least amount of contrition. "As long as I'm on your blacklist, I'll secure my position there by telling you that you're going to dinner with me."

She looked at him incredulously. "You're not only rude, Mr. Rivington, you're demented as well. I'm not going anywhere with you."

"Yes, you are. Doctor Norwood said you would."

27

"I didn't know that Doctor Norwood was running a dating service."

"I told her I wanted to talk to you over dinner. She said she thought that was a very good idea."

"That's far from a directive. She's my employer, not my mother."

"Will you?"

"What?"

"Have dinner with me."

During this exchange Lauri had been straightening the classroom. He stalked her. Each time she turned around, he was standing there. She reached in the bottom drawer of her desk for her purse and slammed it shut as she stood up.

He loomed over her, and she stepped back a half step to increase the small space between them. "You don't listen very well, do you? I said I wasn't going to dinner with you and I'm not. As far as I'm concerned, we have nothing to discuss. You said everything you had to say at our last meeting, and so did I."

He put a restraining hand around her wrist when she tried to push past him. His fingers clasped her in a warm, firm grip that raised the tempo of the pulsebeat beneath them.

"I'm sorry about the unflattering things I said."

He was an actor, she said to herself. He could conjure up any attitude or emotion on a whim. She doubted his sincerity, and her skeptical expression told him so. "I mean it," he said, closing his fingers tighter around her

28

wrist. "I didn't know your excellent qualifications then. I didn't know how experienced you were with working with the deaf. I didn't know that your sister was deaf."

She pulled her arm away with a quick jerk. "Don't ever pity me, my family, or my sister, Mr. Rivington."

"I—"

"My sister is a beautiful woman. She's an accountant."

"I—"

"She is married and lives with her two lovely sons and her successful husband in Lincoln, Nebraska. Believe me, she knows more about the real values of life than you'll ever know."

Her face was flushed with anger, and her chest rose and fell in agitation. The brown eyes that flashed with russet lights were fiery as they smote the man standing so close, he could feel the heat of rage radiating from her.

"Are you finished?" he asked dryly.

She drew several deep breaths and lowered her eyes. His had softened and were more threatening this way than when they were glinting ferociously.

"I wasn't implying pity," he said. "Rather, admiration and respect. Okay?" Her breath caught in her throat when he placed his finger under her chin and tilted her head back. "I've changed my earlier opinion. I think you're exactly what Jennifer needs. What I need."

His words were spoken in the barest whisper. The halls had cleared of students and faculty, and there was an aura of intimacy surrounding them. The expression *what I need* could mean something entirely different in another context. Lauri's heart had responded to that accidental choice of words and was pounding as though demanding release from her chest.

He was too close; the room was growing too dark; the building was too quiet; his breath was too fragrant; and the fingers still holding her chin were too firm and confident. Lauri was choking on her own sensations. Breathing became an overwhelming task. She tried to pull her chin away, but he wouldn't let her. He forced her to look up at him before he said, "You want to take the job."

It wasn't a question. He knew she longed for the challenges and rewards of bringing Jennifer out of her silent world and introducing her to a new one.

"Don't you?" he persisted.

"Yes," she breathed. What was she conceding? Was he leaning toward her or was that her imagination? It must have been, because he released her an instant later and reached for her blazer, draped across the back of the chair. "Let's go get something to eat."

As she shrugged into the jacket he held for her, he asked, "Have you shrunk? You were taller than this the other day."

She blushed slightly to think he had noticed and remembered her height. She grinned up at him engagingly. "I've started wearing sensible shoes." He ran his eyes down the white linen dress, now covered by the navy blazer, to the navy sandals that were much lower-heeled than the shoes she had worn to the television studio.

"Well, I'll be damned. So you have." Ruefully he ran his hand through the silver-brown hair and then laughed out loud as they went down the hall.

He had no trouble hailing a cab, and directed the driver to the Russian Tea Room. "Is that okay with you?" he asked as they settled in the backseat of the taxi.

"Yes, I love that restaurant," she answered honestly.

When they arrived, the maître d' led them upstairs to the more secluded dining room and seated Lauri with obsequious courtesy. She was with Drake Sloan, and apparently that counted for something.

She had noticed several heads turning in recognition as they walked in, and she was suddenly self-conscious in the clothes she had been wearing at school all day. She hadn't considered this a date, and therefore hadn't asked that she be taken home to change before going to dinner.

"I'm sorry I'm not more dressed up. I didn't think I'd be going out tonight."

He shrugged and said, "You look fine," and buried his head in the menu.

Thanks for nothing, Lauri thought as she opened her menu. A few seconds later she heard him chuckle. She looked up to see him watching her. His green eyes were squinting with humor.

"What's so funny?"

"You are. When I tell you you're beautiful, you get mad. And when I don't tell you you're beautiful, you get mad. You'd better watch that expressive face, Ms. Parrish." He lowered his voice and leaned over the table closer to her. "Everyone else does, I can assure you."

She took that as a compliment and saluted him with the Perrier that he had ordered for her. They sipped their drinks—his was a martini—as they commented on the ambience of the dining room. Its dark green walls, deep red trim, and brass appointments radiated elegance without ostentation.

They decided on chicken Kiev and rice. In a few short minutes the waiter arrived with an appetizer of smoked salmon, caviar, boiled eggs, and various relishes. Unselfconsciously Drake began eating with enthusiasm.

"Wait," Lauri said. "You'll have a lesson first." Much to his irritation she made him learn the sign for everything on his plate and all the implements on the table before she would let him continue eating. At one point she laughed. "If there's a sign for caviar, I don't know it. For the time being we'll just spell it out," she said.

Conversation was light throughout the meal. When the table had been cleared and they were sipping cups of coffee, Drake broached the subject of Jennifer.

"You *are* going to accept the job as her private tutor, aren't you?"

She looked down at the table and drew a pattern on

the white linen cloth with the handle of her spoon. "I'm still not sure, Drake."

"What can I do to make you sure?" There was a teasing quality in his voice, but his face was set in serious lines.

"You can promise me that you'll enroll in a sign language class and begin using it constantly. Start thinking in sign, even as you do in English. If I take the job, I'll be Jennifer's surrogate mother for a while. She will depend on me for everything. Someday, you'll have to take over those responsibilities. Will you be ready for them?"

"I'll try to be. I promise to try," he said solemnly. He leaned over the table, worry causing a deep furrow between his brows. "Lauri, what can I expect from Jennifer? What will she be like when she grows up?" It was a vulnerable, concerned father who faced her now.

She saw the familiar pain in his eyes, that longing to know what even the most learned experts couldn't guess. Every parent of a deaf child asked that question.

Lauri measured her words. "She's very bright, Drake. She knows more than she expresses. I think her deficiency is emotional, not mental. I'll incorporate every method of teaching I know. She'll learn sign for basic communication, but at the same time she'll learn the alphabet just as every child does. And she'll learn the sound a particular letter makes. Her hearing aid will help her distinguish speech sounds and patterns. Eventually she'll be able to talk." When she saw his eyes light up with hope, she qualified her last statement. "I want you to understand, Drake, that she'll always be deaf. She'll never hear things like we do. Her hearing aid isn't a corrective device, it's an amplifier."

"I've been told that, but I can't understand it," he admitted.

"Okay," Lauri said. "I'll try to explain. Eyeglasses are for correction. You put on your prescription glasses and you have twenty-twenty vision. The hearing aid only amplifies what Jennifer is capable of hearing in the first place. Suppose you were listening to a radio, but there was nothing but static. If you turned up the volume, you wouldn't hear anything more clearly. You would hear a louder distortion. Does that help?"

He tapped the beautiful white teeth under his mustache with his thumbnail. "Yes. I see what you mean."

"I want Jennifer to know everything. If I took her to the park and demonstrated the verb *to run*, she would learn it and understand it, but that's all that word would mean to her. I want her to know what it means to get a *run* in her stocking, to *run* up a bill, to be tired and *run* down. See?"

"She'll be able to learn that?"

"Only if we teach her, Drake. We've got to talk to her—sign—constantly, just as any child should be talked to constantly. Ellen, my sister, has developed lipreading and speech so well that she seldom even uses sign anymore."

"Jennifer will be able to speak that well?"

"Never as we do," she emphasized. "She'll never hear as we do, so she won't speak as we do. As an actor, you've experienced times when you knew your words of dialogue but couldn't get them out."

"Yeah."

"That's how it is with the deaf all the time. Each word is a struggle. But with proper training and patience, they become quite proficient. Don't expect too much and then you won't be disappointed."

He stared down at his hands, which were now folded on the table. Lauri felt such compassion that she longed to cover those hands with hers and speak words of comfort. Somehow she had to reassure him. "Jennifer can already say my name."

He looked up then and smiled proudly. "Doctor Norwood told me that you two were forming quite an attachment."

It was hard for Lauri to ignore the strings that tugged at her heart each time she entered a room and Jennifer looked up and smiled one of her rare smiles. She felt the same way now as she gazed into Drake's eyes, which looked like liquid emeralds. It was becoming very difficult to remain objective. And that, she knew, was a dangerous situation.

Chapter Three

❧

From the time they left their table until they climbed into the taxi the maître d' had called for them, three different women stopped Drake and begged for autographs.

Lauri was amazed that he could shift his mood so quickly and thoroughly. One minute he had been a confused, concerned parent. The next, he was a confident, arrogant television star, totally in control and in his element as he flashed that famous smile to his adoring public. He spoke to each woman softly, intimately.

The privacy he lent to each conversation must make that woman feel that he actually cared for her. Was he sincere or was he playing a role? It was a disturbing conjecture, and one that Lauri didn't want to dwell on.

"Does that ever get old?" she asked, indicating the

mesmerized woman on the sidewalk. The ardent fan was still clutching to her bosom the napkin that now bore the name Drake Sloan.

"Yes, very. I try to play down the star syndrome and handle the ladies with patience and forbearance. I ask myself, 'Where would I be without them?' That usually puts their ardor into perspective."

Lauri had asked him to return her to the school, as she had some papers there she needed to pick up before going to her apartment a few blocks away.

"Good," Drake said. "I wanted to see Jennifer for a minute anyway."

Lauri quickly checked the gold watch on her wrist. "But it's after nine o'clock. She'll already be asleep."

"Then we'll have to wake her up," he explained blithely.

"Don't any rules apply to you, Mr. Rivington?"

He laughed. "A few. Doctor Norwood knows that sometimes I work at the studio until eight or nine o'clock, depending on the miasma Doctor Hambrick has managed to make of his life that week. So she lets me sneak in a few nights a week to spend some time with Jennifer."

Lauri used her key to let them in a private door that was set to lock automatically after daylight hours. They tiptoed down the shadowed hallway of the dormitory till they reached the room that Jennifer shared with three other little girls her age.

Drake allowed Lauri to precede him into the room, but she stood back when he sat down next to the sleeping child on the bed. He switched on the dim lamp on the bedside table and tapped Jennifer lightly on the shoulder. The child stirred, then opened her eyes and saw Drake leaning over her. She gurgled with joy and sat up instantly, wrapping her arms tightly around his neck.

Lauri hadn't known what to expect, but it certainly wasn't this spontaneous reaction from the child who was usually so constrained and stoic.

"How's daddy's girl, huh? Are you happy to see me?" The question was rhetorical. Jennifer was snuggling against his broad chest while he ruffled her blond curls.

This was yet another Drake Rivington. His features had softened and left no trace of the cynicism that curled his mouth and veiled his eyes. They sparkled with a glow of love when he looked down at his daughter.

When the initial kisses and caresses were dispensed with, Jennifer began searching through his pockets with her tiny fingers and giggling as he playfully shoved them away. Finally she triumphantly produced a package of chewing gum and began unwrapping it.

"Wait a minute, young lady. You can't have that now," Drake said. Then he shrugged and said, "I guess you can," as she successfully peeled the paper from one of the sticks of gum.

"No, she can't," Lauri said quietly but firmly. Drake looked up at her, but, of course, Jennifer hadn't heard this pronouncement. She was just about to pop the chewing gum in her mouth when Lauri thumped the end of the bed to get the child's attention.

Jennifer looked up at her and smiled. Lauri smiled back and signed, *Hello, Jennifer. What is my name?*

Jennifer signed Lauri's name and spoke a facsimile of it in a timid, soft voice. Drake's mouth opened in surprise.

"Sweetheart, that's wonderful," he cried, hugging the little girl closer to him. Jennifer basked in the obvious show of approval from the tall wonderful man who came to her room periodically and gave her special attention. He never talked to the other girls. Only her.

Lauri took advantage of the situation. Getting Jennifer's attention again, she said, "This is Drake," and showed Jennifer the sign for his name that they'd invented. "I'm not sure she understands family relationships yet. We'll have a lesson soon on *father* and *daughter*. For the time being, you'll be simply *Drake*," Lauri explained.

Jennifer made the sign for Drake's name and pointed to him. "Yes," Lauri said, nodding her head. Proudly Jennifer repeated her motions until it turned into a game, and all three of them were laughing. When she started to put the temporarily forgotten gum in her mouth, Lauri stopped her with a gentle tug on her arm. Using what communication devices she thought Jennifer could understand, she conveyed that they would leave it on the bedside table until she woke up.

Hopefully Jennifer looked to Drake for support, but he shook his head, placed the package of gum on the table, and made the sign for *sleep*, which he had noticed Lauri using moments before.

Jennifer yawned and lay back down on the pillow. She looked like an angel with her blond hair and frilly pink nightgown. She clung to Drake's neck as he tried to pull away. He kissed her quickly on the forehead and stood up. Just before he switched off the lamp, Jennifer looked to the foot of the bed and extended her chubby arms to Lauri.

Lauri looked at Drake, who was smiling tenderly. "I think that's eloquent enough," he said. She went to the side of the bed and leaned down for Jennifer's wet, enthusiastic kiss.

They tucked her in for the night, turned out the light, and left the room. Lauri took a few steps, then stopped. Her mind was so full, she couldn't seem to think and walk at the same time. She stood still in the middle of the hallway.

"I think the two of you have just put me through emotional blackmail," she mused.

"That was our intention." Drake's voice echoed her soft, serious tone.

Lauri looked up at him. She spoke her thoughts aloud. "She loves you. You'll be separating yourself from her by moving her across the country. She's very young. Right now you are the most important person in her life. Drake, do you realize that I'll replace you in her affections?"

He looked down the deserted hall, staring at nothing as he slipped his hands into the pockets of his slacks. "Yes," he said, hardening his jaw. "I hate it. If there were any other way—I don't want her to grow up in the city. I can't do for her right now what you can." Then he faced her. "I'm giving you a tremendous amount of responsibility, I know. But I think it's the right thing to do. I'll come to see her whenever I possibly can." He grinned wryly. "I don't lead near the decadent lifestyle the magazines say I do."

She extended her hand in a businesslike manner. "I accept the position you offer." He shook her hand.

He insisted on seeing her to her door when they arrived at the comfortable—but far from luxurious—apartment building. He paid the cab fare, saying he would hail another after seeing her safely inside.

As they rode the elevator up to her floor he said, "I think I can make all the arrangements in about two weeks time. Will that be enough for you?" At her nod he continued. "The house is nice, nothing fancy. I'll buy a car to be delivered to you upon your arrival in Albuquerque. Someone will have been hired to thoroughly clean the house. When you get to Whispers, everything should be ready for you and Jennifer to move right in."

"Whispers. I like the name." His hand was under her elbow as he ushered her out the elevator. He didn't remove it.

"It's a quaint town. A lot of retired people live there, a few mine workers and their families. It's quiet and peaceful. The scenery is gorgeous in every season."

They were standing in front of her door now. Drake said, "I'll pay you whatever the school does. Then of course, you'll have the house and car at your disposal. And I'll give you a generous allowance for food, clothing for Jennifer, whatever you need."

"I'm not worried about money," she said as she inserted the key in the lock.

She turned to tell him a civil good night, but the words were never formed. He moved forward until she was forced to step backward in retreat, until she could go no farther. She was against the wall of the hallway, and he placed his palms flat on either side of her just above her head and leaned toward her. Only inches separated them, but he didn't touch her.

"I like you this way," he whispered.

What had happened to her voice? She couldn't utter the words that came to mind. Finally she managed to gasp "What way?"

"Quiet and congenial and cooperative. But then"— he chuckled—"I liked you the other day, when you were breathing fire at me and so furious that your hair glowed like a torch." He moved even closer. "In fact, Ms. Parrish, I'm trying damn hard to find something I don't like about you."

Instinct told her he was going to kiss her. She knew she shouldn't allow it but was powerless to move as she

43

watched his face come nearer hers. A heartbeat before his lips met hers, she closed her eyes. Though she had known it was going to happen, she wasn't prepared for the onslaught of emotions that rioted through her body at his touch.

The mustache tickled her lips as he brushed it across them. He moved imperceptibly closer until, for the first time, their bodies felt the complementary curves of the other.

They fit together like pieces of a puzzle. She barely reached the middle of his chest, yet they were like two halves of a whole. Her soft breasts were welcomed by his chest as though hollows had been carved out to accommodate them. His feet were on either side of hers, and when his lean, hard hips melded into the womanly softness of hers, a groan born of agony and delight swelled from deep in his throat.

His lips sipped at hers, lingering and then receding until she was tempted to clasp his head and hold it to her. She garnered only the courage to raise her hands shyly to his ribs and lightly caress the muscles just above them. They were bunched and contracted in the effort of supporting him against the wall.

His breath escaped in a long, slow sigh when he felt her dainty hands touching him. His mouth ceased its provocative teasing and descended on hers, claiming it with a precision that was alarming.

Lauri didn't participate at first. Fear and caution had

restrained her responses to men since her disastrous marriage. But Drake didn't countenance that halfhearted resistance. His lips fed hungrily on hers until she parted them and gave his probing tongue the access it begged for. She tried to restore order to the world, to put things back into their proper perspective, but it was impossible under his relentlessly searching mouth.

Even when they had to pause to breathe, he wasn't satisfied. He nuzzled her ear with his mouth and nipped her lobe with his teeth. His hands slipped down the wall to caress her shoulders, her arms, then back to her neck. His fingers seemed to count her pulse rate before moving up to cup her face. His thumbs stroked her cheekbones.

"Do you kiss all your leading ladies like that?" Lauri asked, smiling languidly.

She expected him to smile in return and offer a witty retort. Instead, she watched in puzzlement as his face drained of all color. The green eyes, which had been lighted by an internal fire that seemed to touch her with tongues of flame when he stared down into her upturned face, became cold, impenetrable, as though a curtain had been dropped over them.

He pulled away from her by degrees. First his hands lowered from her face. Then her chest was relieved of the hard pressure of his. When he stepped away from her, she was bereft over his withdrawal and made a motion to reach out and bring him back. But the look on his face stunned and frightened her, and she quickly brought her hands together in a tight fist at her chest. He had gone completely ashen and was staring at her as if he had seen a ghost.

"Drake, what—"

He moved his lips several times before he was able to mouth the words. "S-Susan used to say that." He paused and raked a hand over his face, pushing against his eye sockets, dispelling an image. "She said that all the time."

"Susan?" Lauri queried in a high thin voice. She knew who Susan must be, and she didn't want to hear it.

"Susan was my wife. She died."

He had said it, and with such visible anguish that Lauri was sickened. He still loved his wife! He hadn't said how she died; that was irrelevant. It was her death, not the means of it, that had taken away his love.

"Yes. I'm sorry," she whispered. It was such a lame, worthless thing to say, but she could think of nothing else, and she was desperate to fill the heavy silence that had so suddenly smothered them.

He straightened, seeming to recover from the momentary stupor her unfortunate words had induced. He ran his hands through the silver-brown hair and then said brusquely, "It doesn't matter."

But it did! Only seconds ago she was lost in an embrace that was sweeter and warmer than any she had ever known. Now the man who had made her body sing with sensations she had thought long dead was acting like a stranger—a distant stranger.

His hands were thrust deep into the pockets of his slacks as he turned away from her. When he pivoted on his heels to face her again, his mouth was set in a grim line, and his heavy brows were lowered over his eyes.

"I think it only fair to tell you, Lauri, that I don't allow any emotional entanglements in my life. Despite what you read in the celebrity magazines, I never become attached to any woman. I was married and I loved my wife. My needs are purely physical. I thought you should know that at the outset."

His words were like a brick being dropped on the top of Lauri's head that jarred her to her toes. Rage and humiliation boiled in her veins, and she bristled like a pouncing cat. She tried to control her voice, to trap the deprecations that screamed inside her and craved to be voiced.

"I don't recall asking you to become 'entangled,' Mr. Rivington." She was quivering with suppressed fury. "However, since you have broached the subject and erroneously construed my motives, I will set the record straight immediately. I have no intention of becoming 'attached' to you. In addition to the fact that it would have an adverse effect on my required objectivity, I find you deplorably conceited. I was married to an artist once—a musician—and he, like you, took himself far too seriously and expected everyone else to. You may rest assured that I want the necessary relationship we must have to be strictly professional. Thank you for dinner."

With that she whirled through the door and closed it firmly behind her. She leaned against it, breathing deeply and trying to stem the tears of rage that were already stinging her eyelids.

She heard his footsteps take him to the elevator, heard the bell ring as the doors swished open, then heard them close again.

"Fool!" she screamed to herself, stamping her foot in a reaction that reverted to her childhood. She flung her purse into the nearest chair and virtually ripped off her jacket.

"That supercilious son of a—"

Lauri didn't know whom to direct her fiercest anger against—Drake or herself. She marched to her bedroom, and after switching on the light, she flopped down on the bed and leaned down to unstrap her sandals.

"You never learn, do you, Lauri? You're a glutton for punishment, aren't you?"

As she undressed she continued to castigate herself for submitting to Drake's kiss in the first place. He was her employer. She was responsible for his child. She knew better than to allow emotional attachments to cloud her objectivity. And thinking romantically about Jennifer's father spelled destruction for the child's well-being. Getting so involved with Jennifer was threatening enough to her education. Having sexual desires directed toward the father of the child was the height of lunacy.

It wasn't kissing him that bothered Lauri, but rather the way she had felt while she was kissing him. Not even when she had been so deeply in love with Paul had she felt that helpless sinking feeling she had just experienced under Drake's kiss.

She had been sinking, and then the support had been ruthlessly and selfishly withdrawn. And to add insult to injury, he had had the nerve to suggest sanctimoniously that *she* had initiated the embrace!

Artists! They were all alike. They satisfied their own driving lusts, and after their bruised egos were salved, they trampled on the souls of their healers.

Lauri went into the bathroom and began creaming her face as she recalled her marriage to Paul Jackson. They had met at a party. She hadn't been living in New York long, having just secured a coveted teaching position at the Norwood Institute for the Deaf.

She was lonely, and missed her family, who seemed so far away in Nebraska. When one of the younger, friendly teachers at the school asked her to go to a casual party, she had agreed out of loneliness.

The crowd was a mixture of singles and couples— mostly nine-to-fivers—with a few dancers, musicians, and writers included. Paul Jackson was playing the piano while a leggy blonde sang in a voice far inferior to Paul's accompaniment.

He noticed the red-haired young woman who was standing on the far side of the grand piano and listening to his music with avid interest. When he took a break, he introduced himself, and they began to chat amiably. Lauri was highly complimentary about his playing, espe-

cially when he told her the songs were his own composi-
tions.

It wasn't until months later that Lauri analyzed their
relationship. She realized that, even at that first meeting,
they hadn't discussed her work or dreams or plans. They
had talked exclusively about Paul and his ambitions to
make it big in the music industry. Their first conversation
should have been a clue to his selfishness and insecurity.

He was handsome in a serious, studious way. His
brown hair grew too long, but he rarely thought of getting
it trimmed unless Lauri gently reminded him. Everything
was suggested gently, for fear of offending him or
pricking his inflated self-image.

Perhaps what Lauri had felt for him was pity, but she
convinced herself, after dating Paul steadily for months,
that it was love. He needed her. He needed confidence.
He needed someone to listen to his music and approve.
Encourage. Soothe. Pamper.

"Will you move in with me, Lauri? I need you with
me all the time." They were in his apartment, having
gone to a movie earlier. They were lying on the couch
in a tight embrace.

"Are you asking me to marry you, Paul?" Lauri asked,
smiling. She was thrilled. He loved her. She would be
able to help him, provide him with encouragement, and
be an anchor he could depend on.

"No." He released her and stood up, crossing the room
to the table where he kept his supply of liquor. "I'm

asking you to live with me." He carelessly splashed the whiskey into the glass.

Lauri sat up and adjusted her clothing. He had asked her on many occasions to sleep with him. She had refused, and her refusal usually generated a fight, after which he would apologize sarcastically for asking her to compromise herself.

"Paul, you know I can't do that. I've told you why."

"Is it because your dad is a preacher?" He was becoming more belligerent. His eyes were vacant and glazed.

"Not just that, though my parents would be terribly disappointed—"

"Oh, please," he groaned.

"You know I want to sleep with you!" she exclaimed. "More than anything. But I want to be married to you, not just a live-in."

He muttered an expletive under his breath and tossed down the remainder of the whiskey. He set the glass on the table and stared at her for long moments before crossing the room and kneeling down in front of her.

"You redheaded bitch," he whispered, reaching up to caress her hair. "You know I can't live without this any longer." He placed his hand on her stomach and massaged it enticingly. Then he leaned forward and kissed each of her breasts through her blouse. "I guess I'll have to marry you for it."

"Oh, Paul," she cried, throwing her arms around his neck enthusiastically.

Much to her family's disappointment they were married within days in a civil ceremony, with only two musician friends of Paul's as witnesses. She moved her things into his apartment the next day.

For a month or two, things went smoothly, with Paul having only a few outbursts of temper or periods of abject depression. He was working on a group of songs that he had high hopes for. Lauri came home from work each day to find him at the piano. She cooked meals that he ate abstractedly before returning to his sheets of music.

When she went to bed, he would join her long enough to quickly satisfy his sexual needs, then go back to work while she lay alone in the darkness until she finally fell asleep. Each morning she crept out of bed and left for work without waking him.

When his songs were rejected by a music publisher, Paul went into a state of depression that was fearsome. He drank, cursed, and cried in repetitive cycles.

When Lauri tried to console and encourage him, he screamed, "What in the hell do you know about it, huh? You spend your days with a bunch of dummies who can't even hear music, good or bad. So what makes you an expert, huh? For God's sake shut up!"

He finally came out of the abyss and then went through a period of remorse that was even more irritating than his previous behavior. He cried oceans of tears while she held him in her arms and soothed him like a child. He begged her forgiveness and promised never to speak to her in such a way again. She petted him and nursed him and restored him to a semblance of a rational human being.

But it didn't last.

In the following eight months his fits occurred with increasing frequency. He drank because he couldn't write good music. And he couldn't write good music because he drank. And Lauri suffered for it.

When he was physically capable of having sex, she tolerated an act that was without warmth or affection, but born of his self-anger. She was used as a receptacle for his frustration.

She felt she had to leave him in order to maintain her own sanity and not slip into the questionable category of Paul's stability. She could no longer stand the sudden shifts of mood, the fits of temper, the ego that required continual nurturing, and the paranoia that had to be relieved.

She moved out and took another apartment. She never filed for divorce, still hoping that somehow Paul would overcome his weaknesses and they could love each other as they should.

Three months later he was dead. His current live-in girlfriend called Lauri when she found him slumped over the keyboard of his piano. The autopsy revealed a lethal amount of alcohol and barbiturates; it was ruled an accidental death. Lauri accepted that.

She shook her head sorrowfully now as she pulled the hairbrush through her auburn hair. There had only been a handful of people at the funeral. Her parents had never met Paul. They had not been able to come to New York, and he refused to journey to "a godforsaken place like Nebraska." Lauri had telephoned Paul's mother, who lived in Wisconsin but whom she had never met. The woman listened to Lauri as she explained the details of her son's death, then quietly hung up without saying a word.

At first Lauri had blamed herself for Paul's death. Had she been more understanding, more supportive; had she never left him—maybe he would have pulled himself out of the pit into which he had thrown himself.

It was only after lengthy conversations with her father and the therapeutic passing of time that Lauri stopped her self-flagellation and came to terms with her husband's death.

The marriage had left its mark on her, however. She was cautious about whom she went out with. Young executives who were more ambitious for their careers than they were their love lives were the type she consented to date. Each relationship was left impersonal, and if she felt a man becoming more than casually interested, she retreated with alacrity.

She switched out the light in the bathroom, slipped out of her underclothes, and slid naked under the sheets.

"You've got great luck with men, Lauri Parrish," she chided herself.

She had been so careful in the five years since Paul's death. Aloof and cool, she had allowed no man to matter in her life until now. This wasn't a tiny slipup; this was a headlong plunge in the wrong direction.

Not only was Drake Rivington her employer and the father of her student, but he was an actor! What could be worse than a composer except an actor? Hadn't she just seen evidence of that familiar temperament? One second he was kissing her with a passion that melted her reserves and heated her blood. The next he was cool and distant, drawing away because something she had said reminded him of his deceased wife.

Even more galling was that display of overwhelming conceit. He was accustomed to women fawning over him; panting in expectation of a look, a word, a touch. To hell with that, she thought scornfully as she stabbed a fist into her pillow.

She was launching on a project that might take years and that required—and deserved—her total powers of concentration. She didn't want or need anything, particularly a man, to cloud her judgments. Ignore his taunting arrogance. Dismiss it. Forget him.

Forget that his hair sparkled silver under certain kinds of light. Forget that his eyes were the deepest green, fringed by the darkest lashes, and could pierce one with their intensity. Forget that his body was tall and lean and strong, and that he moved purposefully but gracefully.

Lauri shifted uncomfortably under the covers and ignored the fluttering of her heart as she remembered how Drake's lips felt against hers. Involuntarily her hand went up to her lips, and she touched her mouth, which still tingled from his sweet assault. Her fingers trailed to her ear and the curve behind it that had known the soft caress of his mustache.

She groaned into the pillow and turned over onto her stomach. Other parts of her body longed to be touched, caressed, but she denied them, just as she denied that, despite her resolves to the contrary, she was extremely attracted to Drake Rivington.

Chapter Four

❧

"Jennifer. Jennifer."

The blond curls bounced as the little girl turned her head in the direction of the distorted sound she heard and recognizcd as her name. The hearing aid was hidden beneath the glossy curls.

"Use your napkin," Lauri signed and said as she smiled. "Is it good?" she asked. She was gratified as Jennifer signed *yes* and tried to speak it.

They were in a coffee shop at LaGuardia Airport, waiting for the call that their flight to Albuquerque was ready for boarding. Jennifer was attacking a dish of vanilla ice cream while Drake and Lauri watched her carefully.

"She's improved so much in these two weeks, it's unbelievable, Lauri."

Lauri's heart turned over when Drake spoke her name, but she hid her reaction. "Yes, she has," she answered with an outward calm she didn't feel. She was leaving. She wouldn't be able to see him, even on the impersonal level she had scrupulously enforced on all their meetings since the night he had kissed her.

Maintaining conversation was imperative until she and Jennifer were ready to board the airplane. An uncomfortable silence would be too much to bear. "Remember not to expect too much," Lauri warned.

"I won't," he promised solemnly.

"Yes, you will," Lauri said, laughing, and he returned her deep smile.

The past two weeks had sped by. Drake had managed everything beautifully. He bought out the lease to her apartment, though it was three months until the renewal date. He had made all the travel arrangements and kept Lauri posted on the preparations being made in New Mexico.

She had packed her winter clothes along with Jennifer's and sent them ahead, leaving only their summer things to pack into suitcases at the last minute. What few household utensils she had, she had given away or sold to friends. Drake had told her the house in New Mexico was completely furnished. Her personal items were packed in boxes and checked onto the airplane with her luggage.

Dr. Norwood had been regretful that Lauri was leaving after having been at the school for so long, but she knew how well Lauri was suited to a private-tutoring job and how badly Jennifer Rivington needed that kind of attention. She had wished Lauri good luck and Godspeed.

Lauri had kept all her meetings and telephone conversations with Drake businesslike. Their topics were always about Jennifer or the arrangements being made for the trip and their stay in Whispers.

At their first meeting after the night he had kissed her, he took her hands in his and said quietly, "Lauri, about the other night—"

"No explanation is necessary, Drake." She pulled her hands from his. "I'm afraid we both got carried away by the emotional moment at the school. Please let's not speak of it again."

His eyes had hardened, and the lines on either side of his mouth grew taut, but he didn't say anything. From that time on, his manner had been as clipped and curt as hers. Once, when they were crossing a busy Manhattan avenue at noon, he had clasped her elbow, but immediately released it as soon as they reached the opposite corner. He hadn't touched her since.

Desperately she tried to stifle the wild impulses that raced through her veins each time she saw him. It would be a relief to put half a country between them. She was certain she was only a victim of his charm and good looks that had claimed the hearts of so many. She would get over this infatuation just as she had all the crushes she had suffered through as an adolescent.

"Would you like another Coke?" he asked her now and diverted her out of her reverie.

"No, I'm fine, thank you."

"I think I'll have another quick beer," he said as he signaled a waitress over his shoulder. The poor girl was beside herself as it was, and when Drake turned his attention to her, she nearly stumbled in her attempt to get his drink quickly. Turning back to Lauri, he said, "You said that your father is a minister." She nodded. "Is that why you never drink alcohol?"

Lauri was momentarily taken aback by the question. Then she answered levelly. "No. I used to drink occasionally, socially." She shifted her eyes away from him in a pretense of wiping ice cream from Jennifer's face. "I've seen alcohol do detrimental things to people," she said softly.

"Your husband?" The question was asked in a low voice, but it struck Lauri like a thunderclap. Her marriage hadn't been mentioned since that night outside her apartment.

"Yes," she said, meeting his intent gaze. She sighed. Now was as good a time as any. "I'll tell you about my marriage. Then I never want to talk about it again." Briefly and without emotion or detail, she told him about her short but tumultuous marriage to Paul. "I returned to using my maiden name after he died. I never felt like I really belonged to him nor him to me, so I felt it was hypocritical to use his name."

She lifted her eyes to him slowly. He was watching her closely, touching every feature of her face with his eyes. They alighted briefly on her mouth, and Lauri felt as though she were feeling his kiss again. Then his eyes sought his daughter.

"Jennifer." He thumped the table gently and attracted her attention. He extended his arms and she jumped out of her chair and ran around the table to climb onto his lap.

Drake ignored the beer that the flustered waitress had put in front of him. He held Jennifer tightly, burying his face in her crown of curls. Lauri looked away and blinked back the tears that threatened in the corners of her eyes. She would feel guilty walking onto that airplane with his daughter, separating them.

As he stared down into the child's cherubic face she said, "You might write to her. It will help her realize that you're still a part of her life. I can use the letters as a teaching tool as well. We'll make some trips to the post office, and so on."

"Okay," he murmured, straightening the white knee-socks around Jennifer's chubby legs.

"Of course, we'll become avid fans of *The Heart's Answer.*"

"Oh, God, spare her that." He groaned, but he was smiling again.

The flight was called over the P.A. system in droning, overly modulated tones. For what seemed an eternal moment she and Drake stared at each other across the table while Jennifer chatted to him incoherently. Finally Lauri broke the contact of their eyes and leaned down to pick up the large purse she would take with her on the airplane.

They walked down the concourse silently. Drake carried Jennifer—still innocent of the fact that she would soon be separated from this man, whom she loved with a child's unconditional adoration.

Drake got their boarding passes, and then faced Lauri. "If you need anything, anytime, call me immediately. You're more than an employee, Lauri. I'm putting my daughter in your hands."

"I realize that. I'll do my best for her. You may depend on that." ,

Passengers and airline employees recognized Drake, whispering and nodding. Several women acted absurdly silly, while others merely smiled at him and went on. Lauri was painfully aware of each stare. Drake seemed oblivious to them.

He knelt down and took a package of chewing gum from his pocket. Jennifer reached for it, but he kept it away from her until she asked for it with sign. He hugged her for a moment, then signed *I love you*. She returned the sign, but was actually more interested in the chewing gum.

"Do you think she understands?" he asked Lauri hopefully.

"She doesn't realize that she's leaving you for an extended length of time. She understands love just as any child does."

He seemed satisfied with her answer and nodded absently. His eyes were busy as they perused the crowd waiting to board the airplane. But he wasn't seeing the other passengers any more than Lauri was as she imitated his pretended interest. Eventually his eyes came back to her.

"Lauri," he said hesitantly. He touched her hand that was clutching the boarding passes. He was searching her face again. The green eyes impaled her. They beseeched her to . . . what? She was being drawn into a maelstrom in their fathomless depths. She was drowning.

Don't look at me like that when you're still in love with your wife, she wanted to scream at him. When he made a move to embrace her, she stepped back quickly and took Jennifer's hand. "We'd better hurry. Goodbye, Drake." Before he could stop her, she had gone beyond the gate, showing their passes to an attendant.

Jennifer followed Lauri after one last happy wave to Drake. She had no way of knowing she wouldn't see him again for months. Lauri didn't look back.

She walked on trembling legs through the portable corridor to the door of the jet and located their seats in the first-class section. She made a show of buckling the seat belts so Jennifer wouldn't be afraid of this sudden restriction. The flight attendants were immediately enchanted with the little girl. One of them knew sign language and was soon talking to Jennifer in the child's limited vocabulary.

As the airplane began to taxi Lauri looked back at the terminal and saw through the plate-glass wall the silhouette of a man who could be no one but Drake.

She strove to keep back the tears, which would only upset Jennifer. Her throat was clogged with emotion, and she didn't know if she could tolerate the knifing pain in her chest.

I must fight this, she told herself frantically. *I can't love him. I work for him, that's all.* He's in love with his wife. He's an actor. A soap opera star. He's admitted that any attraction on his part is governed by physical longing and not emotional need. *I don't want him in my life.*

But, even long after the airplane had climbed through the clouds and turned toward the southwest, she still wasn't convinced.

"I couldn't believe that I was finally going to have a neighbor. When Mrs. Truitt—that's the lady who cleaned the house for you—told me that you and the little girl were coming, I was thrilled. Can I help you with any of that?"

Lauri smiled at the plump woman perched on the kitchen stool. Betty Groves lived next door to Drake's mountain home in Whispers, New Mexico.

"No, thanks. If I don't put these away myself, I won't know where they are. I'm almost finished."

Lauri was unpacking cookbooks that she had brought with her from New York. She and Jennifer had been in their new home only one day and were still trying to learn where everything was.

What Drake had described as "nothing fancy," was a far cry from modest. When she and Jennifer had driven up to the two-story Swiss chalet-type house in the new car he had bought for them, Lauri was amazed that anyone could own such a house and not want to live in it all the time.

The lower floor had a large living room, flanked on one side by picture windows looking out on the mountains and on the other side by a stone fireplace. The living room opened into a small paneled room that Drake had suggested she might use as a classroom for Jennifer, and Lauri, when she saw it, agreed with him that it would serve perfectly. A dining alcove was at one end of the living room, and it connected with the cheerful modern kitchen, which also boasted an eating area.

Upstairs there were a huge bedroom, furnished with a king-size bed, an opulent bathroom, another smaller bedroom, and an accompanying bath.

"We may as well enjoy all this room, hadn't we, Jennifer?" Lauri had asked last night as she unpacked Jennifer's bags in the smaller of the two upstairs bedrooms. She would take the larger room. "There's no sense in our living like Spartans, when all of this room is available," she said to herself as Jennifer looked at her new home in silent wonder. She had always lived in the dormitory at school. To her, Lauri thought, this must seem like a palace.

Everything had gone well and with stopwatch precision. She and Jennifer got off the airplane and were greeted by a genial middle-aged man who was delivering the car Drake had purchased over the telephone.

"If you'd rather look at another, Mr. Rivington said I was to work with you until you were satisfied." Lauri looked at the new sleek, silver Mercedes—which sported every option available—and laughed ruefully. "I think this one will be sufficient."

The car salesman helped her pack their bags into the trunk of the car and gave her explicit directions on how to reach Whispers. It was about an hour's drive northwest of Albuquerque.

The house was ready for their occupancy when they arrived. They retired early, after eating a can of soup and some crackers and cheese and unpacking only what they would need overnight.

The first thing that awakened Lauri was the chattering of birds, and she hurried to Jennifer's room, knowing that she would enjoy the morning sights of her new home. The vista was certainly different from the view of Manhattan Jennifer was used to. As Lauri had expected, she was enthralled.

After a large breakfast of bacon and eggs, which Lauri had discovered in the well-stocked refrigerator, she had given Jennifer a bath and dressed her in shorts and a T-shirt. She dressed just as casually and then went to work, finding her way around the house and unpacking the few things she had brought with her.

Betty had arrived with her two children in the middle of the morning. She was bouncy and loquacious, impossible to dislike, and immensely curious.

"I've lived here for three years and never knew who owned this house. No one's ever been here that I know of. Imagine how I felt when I found out that Doctor Glen Hambrick—of course that's not his real name. What is it, again?"

"Drake Sloan is his professional name. Rivington is his real one," Lauri answered with an amused smile. Betty was starstruck.

"Yes! Oh, I nearly *died* when Mrs. Truitt told me that! I was so excited when I found out I was going to have a neighbor with a kid. Then to find out that the neighbor was Glen Ham—I mean, Drake Sloan! Jim may never leave me at home alone again!" she laughed.

Betty seemed to end each sentence with an exclamation point. She had already told Lauri that her husband worked in the mines between Whispers and Santa Fe. He only came home on the weekends, and she was often lonesome for adult companionship.

Betty's two children were as gregarious as their mother. With their black hair and brown eyes they were miniature duplicates of her. She had Sam, who was five, and Sally, who was Jennifer's age. The children had immediately taken Jennifer under their wing and were upstairs in her room playing. Sally had cooed over Jennifer's blond curls and reached out and patted her as she would have a favored doll.

"I hate to disappoint you, Betty, but Drake is still in New York. He won't be living here."

"Oh, I know. But surely he'll come to visit! Do you think you could get his autograph for me? I'd just *die* to have it!"

"I'm sure I could arrange for you to meet him when he comes. If you'd like to," Lauri said goadingly.

"If I'd like to—" Betty broke off with a laugh at herself when she saw Lauri's impish grin.

"His little girl is darling, isn't she?" Betty said after they had shared a minute of laughter. "It's too bad about her being deaf. I didn't even *know* that! And you're her teacher. Just like that lady in *The Miracle Worker*! You sure must be smart, knowing that sign language and all."

"My sister was deaf. I learned sign as early as I learned English."

"Is there a difference?"

"Well, in a way," Lauri answered patiently. "Why don't you and the children learn sign? You could come over each afternoon and I'll teach you."

"You mean it? That would be great. Then the kids could talk—well, I mean—"

"*Talk* is all right," Lauri said.

"Okay, *talk* to Jennifer too."

"Do your children take an afternoon nap?"

"I couldn't stand them if they didn't."

Lauri laughed. "How about each day after naptime?"

"Gee, that's great, Lauri! Thanks." Betty hopped off the stool and picked up one of the cookbooks and thumbed through it. "I'll bet you never eat any of this rich food. You're so thin! I wish I could be tiny and petite like you. You're lucky. When you have babies, you'll probably lose weight instead of gaining thirty pounds like I did. Do you think your skin is the kind that will get stretch marks? My doctor said I wouldn't. I was so mad when I did. You probably won't ever have any. I breast-fed too. A friend said it would be so good for my figure. And it *was* while the kids were nursing. Then, yuk!" She made a derisive gesture with her hands. "They sag! Do you think having a baby will ruin your figure?" Betty asked with candor.

Lauri was fascinated that Betty could talk so fast and change subjects so rapidly, and she listened with awe. When she realized what Betty had asked, she blushed and said quietly, "I don't think I'll ever have a baby."

"Really? I can't imagine not having kids! Doesn't Drake want any?"

"What?" Lauri exclaimed, and dropped the book she had been placing on the shelf above the stove.

"He probably doesn't want any more because little Jennifer was born deaf," Betty said sympathetically. "I guess you can't blame him. Maybe if you talked to him, he'd be willing to have some more."

"Betty," Lauri gulped, swallowed, and finally found her voice. "I'm—we—Drake and I aren't . . . involved. I'm Jennifer's tutor. That's all."

"No kidding!" Betty's round eyes enlarged considerably. "Gee, I'm sorry, Lauri. I just opened up my big mouth and stuck my foot right in. I thought that you two were . . . well, you know. I mean *everybody* does that these days. I didn't mean anything bad. Honest."

Betty looked so contrite that Lauri couldn't help but feel sorry for her. "It's all right, Betty. I suppose to most people it would seem strange that Drake set us up in this house."

"It wouldn't seem so strange if you looked more like Mary Poppins and less like Ann-Margret."

Lauri laughed out loud then, but was instantly reminded of the day she and Drake had first met. It was a poignant memory that caused her heart to twist painfully, and her laughter ceased abruptly. Would she ever get over missing him? It had been only yesterday since she'd seen him, yet it seemed like an eternity. She was relieved when Betty switched to another subject.

The days fell into a pattern. In the mornings Lauri and Jennifer spent several hours in the classroom doing lessons. Lauri was pleased that the child was as bright as she had first judged her to be. Each day opened up new horizons to Jennifer as she learned to communicate with her teacher, whom she believed to be the most wonderful person in the world besides Drake.

Jennifer asked about him daily and never missed an episode of the soap opera. When his image came on the screen, she would shout "Auwy, Auwy," and point excitedly to Drake as she signed his name. Lauri had also taught her what *daddy* meant, and she had connected the two. When she learned *mother*, she asked Lauri if she was her mother. Lauri tried to explain the word *death* by showing her two crickets: one was dead and the other alive. Jennifer grasped the explanation, but Lauri wasn't sure she understood her mother was dead. She had no mental image that associated the word with a person. Maybe she should ask Drake for a photograph of Susan.

They took walks through the foothills that were ribboned with clear streams. Lauri taught Jennifer the signs for everything. It usually took only one time, and the child could remember the word, though they repeated every sign an enormous number of times.

In the afternoons Betty, Sam, and Sally joined Jennifer's sign classes. These were happy times, full of laughter, and the children turned the lessons into a game. Soon they were communicating with Jennifer with the aplomb and unselfconsciousness that only children possess.

"Look, Jennifer," Lauri cried as she opened the mailbox. They had walked down the hill into town to a grocery store to replenish the pantry. "There's a letter in here! I wonder who it's for." As usual Lauri verbalized what she was signing.

"Jen-fa," the child said in her inarticulate but endearing way. She pointed to herself and smiled broadly.

Lauri held the envelope down on her level, and Jennifer pointed out her name, which had been printed in large bold letters. Then she pointed to the name in the upper-left-hand corner. *Drake*, she signed with a giggle.

He had written faithfully to her two or three times a week. Each time the message was brief, but full of love and how much she was missed. And each envelope contained a package of sugarless chewing gum.

He had called them twice, and each time, when Lauri heard his voice, her heart had stopped momentarily, only to begin racing. The conversations were businesslike and to the point. He would inquire about Jennifer's progress, the house, and their basic comforts. He commissioned her to ask for anything she needed and then hung up without one personal word. If he even remembered the kiss they had shared, which Lauri doubted, he didn't show it.

Was it a coincidence that, each time he called, Lauri found it harder to sleep that night? How could the sound of his voice disturb her equilibrium and leave her distracted for the remainder of the day? And at day's end, when she lay in the wide bed alone, her body felt unsettled and dissatisfied. It cried out for—

No! She refused to admit it. But refusing to recognize the obvious was useless.

It cried out for Drake.

Sleeping in the nude was a habit she had acquired during her marriage to Paul. Often when he had left the bed to return to his piano, she had felt too apathetic to retrieve the nightgown he had impatiently stripped from her body.

Her lack of a nightgown had never seemed sensuous—until recently. Now when she lay between the cool sheets, her mind conjured up pictures of Drake. Would he like her this way? What would it feel like to be stroked, caressed, explored by those strong, sensitive hands? Would they seek out that mysterious moisture that both thrilled and alarmed her by its very presence? Would they ease her swollen breasts, which ached with unquenched desire?

She would toss restlessly until her fantasies became dreams. And in the dreams she realized fulfillment.

"Hi. Whatcha doin'?" Betty asked, sticking her head through the back door after an obligatory knock.

"We just got a letter from Drake," Lauri said.

"Ooooh," Betty groaned. "Can I touch it?"

"You silly." Lauri laughed and started unloading the sack of groceries while Jennifer continued to chatter to her letter as though she were talking to Drake.

Betty sat down on the kitchen stool, which had become her usual perch. Since Betty's husband was away so often, the young women spent a lot of time together.

73

Lauri was grateful for the friendship that had sprung up between them, even though their backgrounds were so diverse.

"Hey," Betty said, opening a package of cookies and popping one into her mouth, "I'm taking the kids to see *Sleeping Beauty* this afternoon. Disney, you know? Do you and Jennifer want to come along?"

"Sure. That sounds like fun."

For once Betty hesitated over her words. "I didn't know if deaf kids went to movies or not."

"Of course, they do," Lauri said. "We watch *Sesame Street*, and she learns from it. She can't hear the movie, but it's still light and color and motion. She'll love it."

Jennifer did enjoy the movie. When she had a question, she signed it, and Lauri would answer. Otherwise she was captivated with the masterly animated cartoon. When the witch turned into the dragon, she became frightened; she climbed up into Lauri's lap and hugged her close. Lauri explained that the dragon wasn't real. The explanation seemed to satisfy her for the moment, but Lauri decided she would try to teach her the concepts of *real* and *pretend* in a future lesson.

It had been a long day and Lauri was tired. The movie had taken up most of the afternoon, but she and Betty had taken their time getting home. Jim Groves was staying in the mountains that weekend, so Betty wasn't eager to return to her house with only Sam and Sally for company.

They strolled the hilly, picturesque streets of Whispers with the three children in tow. They stopped at several artisan shops that interested Lauri. Jennifer enchanted everyone she met. In the month they had lived in the small community, she had already made friends with several shop owners. Everyone knew on sight the lovely red-haired woman and the blond, curly-haired child who was always with her.

She and Betty decided to treat the children to hamburgers and milk shakes for their dinner, and then they trudged up the hill toward their houses with the very tired and fractious children tagging behind them.

Jennifer had been bathed and tucked into her single bed in the small bedroom in a matter of minutes. Lauri felt that she had earned a long hot bath in the opulent bathtub.

There was something sensuous and sinfully alluring about this bathroom. The tile floor and walls were pristine white, but in stark contrast the sunken tub was black marble. The basin and shower were of the same material, and the shower door was clear glass, not frosted as Lauri was accustomed to. She felt decidedly wicked each time she showered in full view of the mirrors that lined the opposite wall.

As she sank into the steamy, bubbled water in the tub, she marveled again at its size. It was at least three feet deep and seven feet long. She stretched out her full length and luxuriated in the soothing warmth.

When she finished bathing, she washed her hair and

wrapped a towel turban-style around her head. Deciding she was hungry—she had walked off the hamburger she had eaten earlier—she negligently wrapped a towel around her, tucked the end between her breasts, and went downstairs, careful not to turn on any lights.

In the kitchen she put several cookies she and Jennifer had baked that morning on a plate, poured a glass of milk and put it on another plate, and went back through the door to the living room.

What made her look toward the oversized easy chair she never knew. But her heart leaped to her throat, and she barely bit off a scream. She jerked in such a startled manner that milk sloshed over the side of the glass, and the towel that was wrapped around her slipped precariously lower.

"You'd better be careful or you're going to have no secrets from me," Drake drawled.

Chapter Five

🍂

Lauri wanted to believe that her pounding heart and the liquid weakness that invaded her limbs were generated by fright. But fear was only one catalyst. Another one, stronger and more powerful, was Drake Rivington's presence.

His feet were stretched out in front of him as he slumped in the easy chair. A cowboy hat was pulled down low over his brows, but his eyes pierced the shadows and seemed to gleam from beneath the wide brim. He rolled out of the chair slowly, lazily, with deliberation.

He was dressed in jeans and a denim jacket. Oddly enough, he didn't look like the men who paraded down Fifth Avenue in the trendy new Western clothes straight out of Saks. Drake's were faded and worn, and he looked like he belonged in them.

He advanced like a stalking panther and stopped within inches of her. His nearness was overwhelming. Lauri involuntarily took a deep breath, and when she released it, the towel slipped another notch. She couldn't reach for it and assure its security. One hand held the plate of cookies, the other the glass of milk. If she moved toward a table to set them down, she was afraid the towel would fall away altogether.

Drake realized her predicament and the dimple in his cheek deepened mischievously as he pushed the cowboy hat back with his thumb. "Now, what should I do, ma'am?" he asked musingly. "If I take the cookies, you'll no doubt spill the milk in your haste to grab the towel. If I take the milk, the cookies will slide off the plate, and that would be such a waste. They smell home-made." He leaned down and sniffed the cookies. His head was very close to hers, and the scent of his cologne overpowered the fresh-baked aroma of the cookies and was much more tantalizing.

He straightened and moved a step closer. "On the other hand I could take the towel and solve all our problems," he said gruffly.

Her breath caught in her throat as his hand moved to her cleavage, where the end of the towel had been carelessly tucked in. He settled his index finger on the top curve of her breast. "Did you know," his voice was the merest whisper, "that you have five freckles right here?" He indicated the spot by smoothing his finger across her skin. "That's unusual. Redheads usually have freckles all over. And you only have five. But they are in such a naughty and nice place."

She was captivated by the persuasion in his voice. His fragrant breath fanned her face and seemed almost life-supporting. She wanted to draw it into her own body. Stroking fingers were insinuating their way under the towel. When she felt them pressing the soft curves of her flesh, the fires of desire that had been smoldering in her were doused. Anger superseded passion.

She stepped back quickly and hissed, "You scared me half to death! Why didn't you let me know you were here?"

"Well, I started to, but you were in the bathtub. Would you rather I'd barged into the bathroom to inform you of my arrival? That would've left you without the benefit of a towel," he mocked as his eyes raked over her insolently. "I didn't know you walked around my house like this. I assumed that a nice girl like you would put on a robe or something more modest when she finished bathing."

She ignored the gibe and hung on to his first words. "H-how did you know I was bathing?"

He cocked an eyebrow knowingly. "Now, how do you think I knew?" he asked with an amused glint in his eye. She gasped and blushed to the roots of her hair. "I heard the water splashing," he said casually.

Her reaction was as he predicted it would be. She stamped her foot in anger, and he laughed as she ground out an "Oh!" She had momentarily forgotten the towel, but was reminded of her precarious state when she felt it slip even farther down her breasts until it was barely clinging to the pointed crests.

"Will you please stop laughing and take these out of my hands. I'm cold."

"It's no wonder. Running around naked like that," he teased, but he relieved her of the milk and cookies. She hastily grabbed the towel and secured it in her tight fist, which she longed to smash into his smirking mouth.

"If you'll excuse me, Mr. Rivington, I'll be back shortly, and then I want to know what the hell you're doing here."

"You'd better talk nice to me," he warned. "You still have to climb the stairs. That towel doesn't begin to cover all it should. I can either be a gentleman and turn my head or I can stand at the foot of the st—"

"Will you please excuse me, Mr. Rivington, while I make myself more presentable to be interviewed by my employer?" she asked in a saccharine voice.

"Certainly, Ms. Parrish. I'll be in the kitchen when you come back down."

"I won't be a minute." Without waiting to see if he was looking up the stairs or not—she really didn't want to know—she ran up them and into her bedroom.

Her fingers were trembling as she slipped into a pair of jeans and a flannel shirt. The nights were growing cooler in the mountains.

What was he doing here? Why hadn't he told her he

was coming? She whipped the towel off her hair and brushed it out. It hung in damp tendrils to her shoulders, but was already curling in its naturally soft waves. She didn't take the time to blow it dry. She wanted to see Drake—but only to find out why he had come, she averred to herself.

Her legs seemed to have turned to jelly as she descended the stairs. When she went into the kitchen, he was standing at the range scrambling eggs. Fresh coffee was bubbling in the percolator, and there were two slices of toast in the toaster. His jacket and hat were hanging on pegs by the back door.

"I'm starving. The food on the flight down wasn't fit to eat, and I didn't stop between here and Albuquerque. Did you want something?"

"Yes, I want to know what you're doing here."

He slid the fluffy eggs out of the nonstick skillet onto a waiting plate. He put his hands on his hips and stared at her for several seconds then walked past her on his way to the living room. Lauri followed, exasperated and puzzled.

He went to the front door, opened it, and stepped through. Looking up over the door, he said, "Four-oh-three. Just what I thought. This *is* my house." He came back in and shut the door, ignoring her militant stance as he swaggered back into the kitchen.

"Very funny," she said as she followed him.

"I thought so," he tossed over his shoulder as he opened the refrigerator door. "Do we have any cheese?"

"We?" she asked, stressing the word.

"Okay. Do *you* have any cheese, Ms. Parrish?"

She couldn't meet the teasing eyes that looked at her over the refrigerator door. "In the bottom drawer," she muttered, looking down at her bare feet. Had she forgotten to put on any shoes?

"How's the strawberry jam?"

She was totally disconcerted. "What?" she asked impatiently.

"We've—I'm sorry, *you've* got grape, apricot, and strawberry jam. Do you recommend the strawberry?"

That did it.

"Will you please stop with this inane chatter and fix that damn plate of food and sit down so I can talk to you?"

She tapped her foot in consternation and folded her arms across her chest. It was then she realized that she hadn't taken the time to put on any underwear either.

"Okay, okay," he said testily, setting his plate on the table. "You never did win Miss Congeniality, did you?" He poured a cup of coffee and asked her with an inquiring lift of his eyebrow if she wanted any. She shook her head negatively.

When he sat down and began wolfing down the food, without any effort to start a conversation, she slunk to the chair opposite him and flopped down with emphasis. He didn't even look at her. *Well*, she thought, *I'll be damned before I ask him anything more.*

When the plate was clean, he wiped his mouth on a paper napkin and took a long drink of the cooled coffee.

"Is the house satisfactory?" he began.

She hadn't expected him to start with a discussion of the house. "Yes," she answered succinctly. When he raised his brows threateningly, she relented somewhat. After all, he was her employer. "It's more than satisfactory. It's beautiful, and you know it. Whispers is a perfect atmosphere for Jennifer. She's learning so much, and the people around here are kind and unhurried."

"How is she, Lauri?" All his teasing and bantering had stopped. He was serious. Lauri tried to ignore the tickling sensation in her midsection that his saying her name had caused. She tried equally hard not to stare with such fascination at his mustache. It had played a integral part in some of her daydreams.

She averted her eyes and answered thoughtfully, "She's fine, Drake. Truly. She's intelligent and witty. Her lessons are going faster than I ever dreamed they would. Her speech is still very slow, but it's coming. Her sign vocabulary and the command of it has quadrupled since we left New York." She smiled then and prodded, "How's yours?"

He signed that he went to class three nights a week and was learning as quickly as a tired thirty-five-year-old man could learn anything.

She laughed. "Very good! You and Jennifer can have discussions on all sorts of things now."

"Are you missing New York?" he asked with a frown.

"No," she answered slowly. *I miss only you*, she thought. When she saw his skeptical expression, she added, "We have a very good neighbor who, by the way, is a big fan of yours and will probably be storming the house when she learns you're here. She has two children who play with Jennifer."

He seemed surprised and asked, "Are they—I mean, do they—" He groped for the words, but Lauri supplied them.

"Do they treat her like a freak? No, Drake," she assured him. "They treat her like they would any other playmate. They have their squabbles and times of affection just like any other children. Betty and the kids are learning sign. They can talk to Jennifer quite well now."

"That's good," he said, nodding into his coffee cup. It was almost sad to see him so relieved. Lauri stymied the impulse to reach out and touch the silver-brown hair that was tousled from having been under the cowboy hat. The fine lines around his eyes seemed more deeply etched, as if he hadn't been sleeping well. Did he miss his daughter that much? Or had coming to Whispers reminded him of the time spent here with Susan? The pain of that thought was intolerable. Lauri could feel that her features were displaying her emotions, and she quickly masked them.

"How long will you be in Whispers?" she asked.

He brought his head up and looked at her a moment

before standing and crossing to the coffeepot to refill his cup.

"Indefinitely," he said.

She stared at him in surprise. What did he mean by *indefinitely*?

"I don't understand," she said.

He took a sip of coffee and turned back to face her. "I have a helluva headache. Would you make yourself useful and give me a neck rub?"

That swift change of topics took her completely off guard. Instinctively she nodded and walked around behind his chair as he sat down. Cautiously she placed her hands on his shoulders near his neck and gently squeezed the tense muscles under the cotton shirt that was stretched across them.

"Ah, thanks. That feels great." He took another sip of coffee. When he began talking, he sounded introspective. "I got fed up with that crap I was having to do and say on that soap. I'm tired of it. In seven years I've had four marriages and innumerable affairs, and a car wreck in which I lost my memory. I almost married my long lost sister before we discovered our kinship. I lost my son to leukemia, and had my medical license revoked because a rich man's daughter accused me of aborting a fetus that she claimed was mine. I'm sick to death of Doctor Hambrick. Seven years of scripts like that are enough."

"You mean you quit?" she asked aghast, and abruptly stopped rubbing his neck just behind his ears.

"Not exactly. Please don't stop." When her fingers resumed their work, he continued. "I told Murray that I wanted to get away for a while and get my head together. I've only had a few days vacation in all this time, so I was due several weeks. Wednesday of this week, we taped an episode where Doctor Hambrick gets knocked over the head by a mugger while he and his lady love are strolling through Central Park. He's in a deep coma. She was raped, so all the attention will be on her for a while. She'll no doubt fall madly in love with another doctor," he remarked with a derisive snort.

"They swathed my head in bandages, put me in a hospital bed, and shot a few minutes of tape while I lay there motionless. Anytime they refer to Doctor Hambrick, they'll splice in that piece of tape. And while they do, I'll be here with Jennifer enjoying autumn in New Mexico."

"You can do that?" Lauri had only a vague idea of the powers of network television and thought that Drake was taking a dangerous gamble as far as his career was concerned.

He only shrugged. As he did, his head fell back against the cushion of her breasts. Her fingers traced up his jaw, over his temples and rubbed rhythmically. One might imagine that she was holding his head against her, but she knew better.

"For a while," he said, finally answering her question. "In all humility I've kept that show afloat for several years. I've got a few strings I can pull. Besides, everyone knows how temperamental we actors are." He was joking, but the words struck Lauri like a slap in the face. *Yes, I know,* she thought.

To change the subject she asked, "Where will you be staying?"

He laughed and tilted his head back to look at her, an action that caused her breath to catch in her throat. Did he realize what he had just moved against?

"Where will I be staying?" he mocked. "Well, my room is the large one upstairs. The one with the king-size bed and the mirrors on the closet doors."

Lauri jumped away from him as if she'd been shot. Her mellow mood of a few minutes ago was completely dispelled. "You can't mean that you're staying here!"

"I'm sure as hell not checking into the Mountain View Motel, Ms. Parrish," he said sarcastically. "Of course, I'm staying here."

"But you can't. Not with me living here. We'd be—" She licked her lips nervously and clasped her hands together. "You just can't, that's all." Her words sounded childish, even to her.

"Did you start to say that we'd be living together?" He could barely control the humor in his voice. "Yes, I guess we will. In a manner of speaking."

"That's impossible!" she cried.

"Why?" he asked with feigned innocence. Then his green eyes narrowed suspiciously. "Ms. Parrish, I'm

surprised at you. You weren't attaching any illicit conno-
tation to the situation, were you? You wouldn't take
advantage of me, would you? Am I in danger of being
compromised?"

"No. You're certainly not!" she exclaimed coldly.
"Not by me anyway. But you are in danger of being
locked up in an insane asylum if you think I'll go on
living in this house while you're here. If you stay, I'll
have to leave."

"No, you won't," he said confidently as he stood
up and flexed the shoulder muscles she had soothed.
"Jennifer needs you, and you love her too much to desert
her. By the way, I want to see her. Is she in the small
room upstairs?"

With characteristic arrogance he dismissed her argu-
ments as if they were nothing and walked calmly out
of the kitchen, leaving her standing in the middle of the
room, seething with impotent rage.

He was right, of course. She wouldn't leave Jennifer.
She had only now won the child's complete trust and
affection. If she left, Jennifer might suffer irreparable
psychological damage. It was crucial to her development
and education that Lauri stay with her and continue as
they had been.

But she couldn't live here with Drake! She couldn't
reside with any man and remain detached. But to live
under the same roof with Drake, who could melt her
with one touch, one look, would be unthinkable. His
provoking conceit would keep her temper perpetually

agitated. What kind of masochistic torture was she subjecting herself to by staying?

But she would stay. She had known it all along, and so had he. Her only rationalization was that he would soon tire of the quiet life in Whispers and be clamoring to return to New York. Until then she would stay away from him as much as possible. Surely he wouldn't be here long. A week? Two?

She walked up the stairs slowly and went into Jennifer's room, where the night-light provided soft illumination. Drake was sitting on the bed with Jennifer clasped tightly in his arms. He was rocking her back and forth, patting her on the back. Lauri withdrew and went into the bedroom that Drake would now use. She began gathering up a few items to take downstairs with her.

"What are you doing?" The deep voice startled her. She turned and saw him lounging in the doorway.

She avoided his eyes and his question as she asked, "Did she go back to sleep?"

"Yeah," he chuckled. "I don't think she really woke up, but now she knows I'm here."

Lauri nodded and turned to pick up the clothes she had laid out on the bed. "What are you doing?" he repeated.

"I'm getting out of your way," she answered. "If you can wait till the morning to unpack, I'll move my things downstairs then. I'll only take what I need with me now."

"That isn't necessary. Leave everything where it is," he said sharply.

"But I told—"

"I'll sleep in the room downstairs. There's no sense in your moving again."

"But this is your room, Drake. I wouldn't feel right taking it, since the other one is so small."

"I'll adjust. Besides," he said, sauntering into the room, "I like the idea of having you in my room. In my bed." His voice had become husky as he came nearer. It intimated that he would be in that bed too. Lauri's blood pumped like molten lava, and her legs were barely able to support her when he reached up and cupped her head with his hands, sliding his fingers under her hair.

"Your hair is almost dry," he whispered. "I liked it wet too." He caressed her cheek with his lips. "Don't think that bulky shirt hides your figure. I know exactly what your breasts look like, after seeing them covered by only that inadequate damp towel."

His lips toyed with hers, tuning them as one does an instrument before a concert, preparing them for his complete possession. When it came, her lips were ready, and welcomed the indelible imprint he branded onto them that seared into her soul.

His hand moved languorously down her spine to the small of her back. Pausing first for a brief massage, it slipped to her hips and drew her against him. The contact with his body left no question in her mind about his driving desire. Answering with a natural, reciprocal need, Lauri rubbed against him and heard him gasp with pleasure.

Thrusting all her previous caution aside, she matched his kiss with unreserved ardency. Her tongue and lips couldn't taste enough of him. When he lifted his head to caress her cheek with his free hand, she raised up on tiptoe and, with the tip of her tongue, outlined his upper lip just below the brush of his mustache.

"Lauri," he moaned, before he captured her mouth again and searched each secret crevice with an insatiable tongue.

His hand slipped down between their bodies and caressed her collarbone with sensitive fingers. Then they traveled lower until he encountered the first button of her shirt. He opened it expertly and smoothed the top curve of her breast, made more pronounced by being pressed against his chest. His fingers were warm velvet against the honeyed satin of her skin. Under his manipulation, the second button fell away as easily as the first.

Lauri breathed his name when he buried his face in the hollow of her neck and covered her breast with the palm of his hand. He stroked it, pressed it, teased it, until it throbbed with an aching that spread to the center of her body.

Cupping the soft mound, he lifted it free of her shirt. He held it in his hand like a precious treasure. "I adore these freckles," he whispered and lowered his head. He paid them far more homage than they warranted. The kisses he planted into her flesh made her head reel, and she laced his hair with frantic fingers, pulling him closer.

The tickling mustache and nibbling lips rid her of the ability to think, to reason. She didn't want to emerge from this euphoria. She wanted to stay in it until she knew the full glory of making love to Drake.

As if reading her mind, he settled his lips a breath away from that bud on her breast that was desperate to feel the dewy touch of his tongue, but had to be content with the caressing mustache.

"Lauri, let me know your sweetness," he pleaded. "Now. Please. I need your softness. I want you."

His words pierced through that cocoon of sensuality he had spun around her and stabbed through her brain like a laser beam.

Need. Want. Yes, he wanted her. His physical reaction to their embrace was all too evident when he held her this tightly. Why then did she hesitate to surrender completely?

His avowal that he wanted no emotional attachments had brooked no speculation to the contrary. What he wanted and needed wasn't Lauri Parrish the person, the spirit; he wanted her body—and only that. He needed a cradle for that masculine force whose entreaty for release was inexorable. Should she grant him that, his need would be appeased. But there would be no outpouring of thoughts—or feelings—of the essence of the man himself.

Drake Rivington didn't love her. He still loved his wife. The one time he had spoken of Susan, the personal pain of his loss was heartbreaking in its intensity and embarrassing for the one who witnessed it.

As much as she wanted him, she couldn't take him on those terms. But how could she refuse him now? Her desire was all too real. He held her virtually naked and pliant in his arms. His deft fingers were loosening the remaining buttons of her shirt. He would never believe that she had suddenly come to her senses and developed a guilty conscience. Her only recourse was to feign anger. *That* he would believe.

And in a way she was angry. She hated herself for not being able to accept him on any terms when her body longed for him. But she had been down that treacherous road before. Paul had used her sexually as a balm for his pain, his agony. What about hers? Who had been there to ease her suffering?

Never again.

"Drake, Drake," she strangled out and used what little strength her resolve provided her to push him away. "No."

His eyes were glazed with passion, and it took a moment for him to clear his head and realize that she was forbidding him cessation of a physical torment.

"What's the matter?" he asked, still stunned by her unexpected denial.

She buttoned her blouse with clumsy fingers as she stepped away from him and turned her back. "I can't— I don't want to sleep with you," she said euphemistically.

"Like hell you don't," he said, lunging for her. She eluded him and held up hands that warded him off. "Don't you touch me again. I meant what I said," she said in a rush.

His eyes glinted like green ice. He was understanding her now. "And I meant what I said," he growled. "You want me as much as I want you."

"No, I don't," she said heatedly.

"Your body says otherwise, Lauri," he said with captivating serenity. "I can *feel* how much you want me. My hands have brought you to a fevered pitch of craving, and my mouth can do more."

"No—"

"And I want to do more. I want to do everything. I want—"

"Sex!" she interrupted him with an exclamation she hoped would override his seductive language. "I resent your thinking I would be so willing to give myself to you when you've made it eminently clear that you want nothing but sex from a woman." She took several deep breaths.

"I said I wanted no emotional entanglements. That doesn't mean when I hold a very beautiful and desirable woman that I wouldn't like making love."

"Love!" she cried. "You said you loved your wife—"

"Leave my wife out of this," he snarled.

His reaction was so feral that Lauri took a backward step. She should have known better than to taint his wife's memory by bringing her into this sordid discussion. That thought made her angry, and she raised her chin in defiance.

"I'm not one of your fluttering admirers," she said scathingly. "I'm your employee—and I expect you to treat me as such." She hoped her words held more conviction than she felt. Even now, with his hair in disarray and his clothes rumpled from her exploring hands, she wanted to run to him and beg him to kiss her again. She couldn't let him know that. She held the muscles of her face rigid.

"All right," he said tightly. "Even Doctor Hambrick hasn't resorted to rape, and Drake Rivington doesn't have to." He turned away and strode toward the door. Before he went through it, he faced her again with a smirk curling his lip. "Don't feel too victorious. You want me, and I'll have you yet. It's only a matter of time."

He closed the door with more force than was necessary.

Chapter Six

❦

*H*ow dare he talk to me like that! Lauri kept thinking.

She had thought a night's sleep might mitigate some of her anger over Drake's departing words, but she found upon awakening that her fury had only increased. He had caught her vulnerable and unawares with his sudden arrival. He was charming, devastatingly handsome, virile, and accustomed to women falling all over themselves for him.

Well, he'd soon learn that Lauri Parrish wasn't susceptible to his charm. It would be a cold day in hell before she would fall into bed with Drake Sloan.

She wore a look of grim determination when she descended the stairs and walked toward the kitchen. A cursory glance in Jennifer's room had verified Lauri's prediction that the little girl would already be awake and in the company of her father.

She pushed open the barroom doors that separated the kitchen from the dining alcove and strolled with affected nonchalance into the sunlit room. The scene that greeted her was too tranquil and pleasant to perpetuate anger, and the rebellion slowly seeped out of her, gradually deflating her like a leaky balloon.

"Good morning," Drake said in sign as well as verbally. "Jennifer is having cereal for breakfast, and I'm having toast and coffee. What do you want?" God, he was gorgeous, Lauri thought. His hair sparkled with silver lights from the sun that was streaming through the window. The sleeves of his sport shirt were rolled up to his elbows while the shirttail had escaped the confines of his jeans. The threat she had seen on his face when he left her last night had been replaced by a dazzling smile that was even more disarming.

"Good morning," she said and then leaned down to hug Jennifer who was scooping spoonfuls of cereal into her mouth.

She turned to Lauri excitedly and said in sign, "Daddy is here, Lauri."

"I know," Lauri answered. "Do you feel sad?"

"Noooo," said Jennifer. She liked to say that word and it was easy for her, so she dragged it out.

"Are you mad?" Lauri asked. They had had a lesson on basic emotions a few days ago, and Lauri was putting her student through a test.

Jennifer giggled and said, "Noooo."

"Then how do you feel about Daddy being here?"

Jennifer paused a minute and groped for the right sign in her mind. "I am happy," she said, and laughed as Lauri applauded the correct sign. Then she asked her teacher, *Are you happy that Daddy is here*?

Lauri straightened up quickly, hoping that Drake wasn't watching. He was. His thick, expressive brows raised in query.

"Well? Answer Jennifer. Are you happy that I'm here?"

He had put her on the spot. Jennifer was looking up at her with eager expectation. Grudgingly she signed and said, "Yes. I'm happy that Drake is here." Jennifer was satisfied and went back to her cereal.

"You may want to check her hearing aid. I'm not sure I put it in right," he said. Lauri lifted Jennifer's curls and checked the placement and volume gauge on the aid, which was molded into Jennifer's ear. "It's fine," she said.

"Good. What do you want for breakfast?" he asked as he liberally spread butter on the toast.

"I don't eat breakfast," Lauri said. "Coffee is enough for me."

His eyes traveled the length of her body in a perusal that made her blush hotly. "Is it abstinence that keeps you so trim?"

Retreating from his knowing eyes, she went to the countertop and poured coffee into a mug that shook in her trembling hand. As he passed her on his way to the table, he slapped her playfully on the rump, resting his palm against the firm flesh for a moment longer. "Abstinence from too many pleasures can make you nervous, grouchy, and old beyond your years."

She had a perfect retort on the tip of her tongue, but Betty chose that time to fling open the back door and bounce through it with her usual exuberance. Pink curlers were radiating from her head at varying angles. The quilted robe had been secured at her thick waist with a careless knot. Furry slippers increased the size of her feet to an alarming proportion.

She halted and stood stock still when she saw Drake sitting at the table. Her wide brown eyes stared and her mouth opened and closed like a fish washed ashore. If her expression hadn't been so comical, Lauri would have felt compassion for her friend.

She was biting back laughter as she introduced them. "Betty Groves, this is Drake Rivington. Drake, this is the neighbor I was telling you about."

"Good morning, Mrs. Groves," he said, standing and going toward Betty with an outstretched hand. Betty raised her hand like an automaton and Drake shook it lightly. "Lauri's told me what a help you've been to her and Jennifer. I want to thank you for looking after my girls in my absence."

Lauri gasped at the implication, but before she could protest, Betty groaned loudly, "Oh, my God! I look terrible! I just ran over to borrow a cup of sugar. I had no idea you would be here, Doctor Ham—Mr. Sloan—Mr. Rivington. Why didn't you tell me he was going to be here, Lauri?" she asked accusingly.

"I di—"

"You look lovely, Betty. May I call you Betty?" Drake interrupted Lauri before she could defend herself. "Where's our sugar, Lauri?"

Our? My girls? He was doing everything in his power to make it seem like they had set up housekeeping together. She shot him a deadly look over Betty's shoulder, but his eyes only shone with amusement and were free of contrition.

"It's in the pantry," she answered frostily. Neither Betty nor Drake noticed.

"Would you get some for Betty, please, while I pour her a cup of coffee," he said offhandedly as he escorted the enamored Betty to the table. He was playing his charming-celebrity role and Lauri was disgusted by it.

"You look just like yourself," Betty simpered as she sat at the table under Drake's direction. "Really, I shouldn't take up your time. My kids are waiting—"

"Please, as a favor to me, share a cup of coffee." Drake's practiced smile would have talked an angel out of its wings. "Didn't Lauri tell me last night that you had two children?"

Last night! Lauri was furious. As Betty launched into her favorite subject, Drake glanced at her and smiled wickedly. He knew he had intimated that they had spent the night together, and not in separate rooms. She fumed as she slammed cabinet doors getting Betty's cup of sugar.

Betty finally took her leave, promising Drake that she and Sam and Sally would be back later in the day to take their sign lesson. For once Lauri was glad to see her neighbor leaving. She was highly irritated by Betty's fawning over Drake and his subtle suggestions that their relationship was what Betty had at first suspected and which Lauri had vehemently denied.

"While you and Jennifer are in the classroom this morning, I'll unpack my stuff." Lauri had noted there was another car parked in the driveway next to the Mercedes. Drake explained that he had rented it and would return it to Albuquerque when she and Jennifer could spare a day to go with him and drive him back.

She had started Jennifer on a project in the classroom when Drake appeared in the doorway. "Lauri, the closets in that room were built for Munchkin clothes. Can you spare me some space in one of the closets in the master bedroom?"

She looked at him suspiciously. "Is this a ruse, or do you really need the space?"

"I really need the space," he said with the guilelessness of a saint. Then flashed her a brilliant smile that dimpled his cheek. An actor. He could conjure up any expression or mood on a whim. But in spite of herself she smiled back.

"One of the closets is empty except for some boxes stacked at one end. I'll move them, if you like."

"Don't touch them," he snapped.

She was already getting out of the chair that was on the same low level as Jennifer's. She jerked her head up at his harsh tone and saw that his face had lost its previous radiance. It was set in firm, unyielding lines. When he saw her stunned surprise, he said quietly, "Some of Susan's things are packed in them. Leave them alone."

Lauri went frigidly cold. For excruciating seconds everything in the world stopped, only to start revolving again—but without enthusiasm, belatedly, and laboriously.

"Of course, Drake," she stammered. "I only—"

She was talking to air. When she looked up, the doorway was empty.

It was usual for Lauri and Jennifer to stay in the classroom all morning except for a brief break when Jennifer ate a snack. Lauri used this time for teaching as well. Jennifer learned the names and tastes of different foods.

One week they would study cherries. She learned the sign, the written word, and in speech class Lauri would teach her the sounds. She would have cherry Jell-O, cherry juice, cherry candy. She learned to associate a particular taste and smell with the name.

When Lauri and Jennifer left the classroom that day shortly after noon, Drake had already fixed them a lunch of sandwiches and soup. Sitting on the table amidst place mats and napkins was a fluffy pink stuffed bunny. Jennifer squealed and dashed across the room, clutching the toy with rapture.

"I think you've scored a hit," Lauri said.

"I thought she'd like it," Drake smiled at his daughter.

Lauri knelt down beside Jennifer. "What is your bunny's name?"

Jennifer looked at her blankly. She stroked the bunny's exaggerated, floppy ears and mumbled. Lauri spelled out *Bunny*.

Jennifer nodded and laughed, forming the letter signs with her short fingers and thumping the bunny on the head.

"I think he's been dubbed," Drake said.

He remained loving and gentle with Jennifer, but aloof to Lauri. He was moody and quiet during the meal.

What had she expected? Inadvertently she had reminded him of Susan and that had triggered his depression. She had often seen Paul go into a shell and brood about the house for days like Hamlet or some other tragic hero. Paul's bad mood had forced her to calculate each word, weigh everything she said or did in fear of offending his tenuous self-esteem.

Well, she wasn't going to get into that rut again. She gave Jennifer her total attention and ignored Drake. When Betty and her children came over later in the afternoon for their sign class, Drake joined them around the kitchen table.

He was a different person from the sulking figure who

had served lunch. He clowned and joked; his smile was winning; his eyes twinkled with mirth. How could he change so drastically within a matter of hours?

Then Lauri remembered his craft: that's what he was paid to do. He could switch emotions as quickly as one could change clothes. Paul could appear sober and energetic when he was meeting an agent or a record producer, then sink into a fathomless depression on the way home.

She didn't like these sudden shifts in Drake's moods; they made her wonder which person was real. How much could she trust anything he said? Anything he did? When he kissed her, was it real to him or was he only playing a love scene? She had seen him kiss the actress in the studio, and it had been most convincing.

She resolved never to let it happen to her again. Their embraces meant nothing to him, but to her they were vitally important. And the importance she was assigning them was frightening.

These thoughts lingered in her mind as she conducted the sign class. Little did she realize that she had been staring at Drake for long moments, and he was aware of it. When she shook herself out of her reverie, his eyes were on her. She tried to look away, but was held by his magnetism. Her russet eyes focused on him, and for a fleeting second, she knew he read her longing in them.

He signed, *I haven't forgotten the freckles*. His eyes dropped unerringly to her breasts and Lauri felt a ridiculous compulsion to cover them with her hands.

She blushed and looked quickly at Betty and the children, hoping that they hadn't seen or understood. They were involved in a discussion about buying new shoes.

Involuntarily her head swiveled back to Drake, whose lips were curved in an insolent smile under the mustache. *Do you have any others I should know about?* he signed.

No! she answered emphatically with a shake of her head.

I'd like to look for myself, he signed with a command of the language that was suddenly disconcerting. He was becoming far too adept at this form of communication. But he didn't even need his hands to transmit his thoughts. His eyes signaled the message.

She glanced at the others, but the children were naming the animals in a book, and Betty was looking up a word in the sign dictionary.

Will you stop this? Lauri demanded silently with her hands.

Will you let me search for all those secret places of your body? And when I find them, will you let me touch them? Kiss them?

Heat washed over her like a scalding flood. Her heart pounded in her chest and stirred the T-shirt that covered it. Drake saw that agitation and stared at her breasts as they rose and fell rapidly with her unsteady breathing. His eyes came back to hers, and his eyebrows prompted an answer by arching over his eye in a sharp curve.

No! She shook her head, licking her lips nervously. The motion intrigued him as he watched her tongue disappear into her mouth. His look told her he would like to follow it with his own.

Then I'll just have to fantasize about all those hidden places, he signed, and the emerald eyes impaled her as if they were doing just that. *I have a vivid imagination.*

Lauri was grateful when Jennifer distracted her by tugging on her arm. "Auwy, Auwy," she said and pointed down to her tennis shoe, which had become untied.

"Yes," Lauri said absently and turned away.

"Auwy," Jennifer said with more determination and a touch of petulance.

Lauri only looked down at the shoe and nodded, but did nothing and became busy with stacking the books they had used for the lesson.

"Auwy!" This time the tugging on Lauri's arm was demanding and Jennifer's voice was high and whining.

"She wants you to tie her shoe," Drake said impatiently.

Lauri looked at him with composure, though she didn't appreciate his interference in what she considered to be her domain.

"I know what she wants, Drake. I want her to ask me to tie her shoe in a complete sentence."

"Is that always necessary?" he asked. The harsh tone of his voice indicated that he didn't think so.

"Do you want her to learn to talk or do you want her to go around pointing at things and grunting all her life?" she fired back at him. The lines around his mouth tightened, but he didn't say anything more.

Jennifer was on the verge of tears and still tugging at Lauri's arm. Sam and Sally and Betty stared at this tense scene. For once none of them had anything to say.

"Let's go on with the lesson," Lauri said calmly and continued to ignore Jennifer except for glancing down at the shoe and nodding in confirmation that it was indeed untied.

Jennifer, in a fit of temper, fell to the floor, kicked the leg of Lauri's chair, and buried her golden head in her arms.

"Sam, tell us about your puppy in sign," Lauri instructed. "What color is he?"

Sam looked down at Jennifer in sympathy and then glanced uncertainly at his mother. She nodded at him and he started hesitant motions that told the others about his dog. His heart wasn't in it. Indeed, everyone was distracted by the little girl on the floor who was whimpering pathetically.

"Lauri, for God's sake—" Drake started just as Jennifer rose abruptly and stood beside Lauri's chair again. *Lauri, tie my shoe*, the child signed. When Lauri still didn't move, Jennifer rubbed her chest in a circular motion in the sign for *please. Please*, Jennifer added.

Lauri smiled, picked her up into her lap, and hugged her hard. "I want to tie your shoe, Jennifer. But you must ask me. How will I know what you want if you don't ask me?" Jennifer had understood the signs and she flung her chubby arms around Lauri's neck. When she pulled away, she signed, *I love you, Lauri*, and said her teacher's name.

I love you too, Lauri signed and kissed the top of Jennifer's head.

Betty and the children seemed immensely relieved and started chattering at once. Drake said nothing, but Lauri met his eyes over his daughter's head. The green eyes seemed challenging and vaguely envious. But in Lauri's eyes her message was clear: Don't interfere again.

When the next clash came a few days later, it carried even greater force than the first.

Lauri had written a letter to her parents right after breakfast. She wanted to get it in the mailbox before the postman came. Explaining to Jennifer that they would start classes later that morning, she sent her up to her room to play. Drake was puttering around in the backyard.

Lauri finished her letter, put it in the mailbox, and went upstairs to fetch Jennifer who, she suddenly realized, had been mysteriously invisible and extraordinarily quiet for the last half hour.

Jennifer wasn't in her room, and Lauri knew she wasn't downstairs. As she went into her bedroom she could hear soft murmurings coming from the bathroom. Stepping through the door, she gasped at the sight that greeted her.

Jennifer had opened each container of Lauri's makeup, sampled it, applied it to her own face, and then left it opened and ravished on the dressing table. Her cherub face looked like an artist's palette. Eyeshadows, eyebrow pencils, and mascara had all been applied to her eyes in ghastly quantities. Her cheeks and forehead were painted with blushers, lip glosses, and makeup bases in varying shades. Lotions, creams, and powders were either smeared or dusted over the marble top of the dressing table, creating a disgusting, if fragrant, mess.

When Jennifer saw Lauri's face in the mirror, she knew that playtime was over. Unsuccessfully she tried to recap a jar of night cream that she had liberally applied to her knees. Vainly she picked up a Kleenex and tried to clean off the dressing table. When she made no progress, but only managed to spread the mess to a larger area, her bottom lip began to tremble, and she looked up at her teacher suppliantly.

"Jennifer," Lauri said sternly, "this was naughty! It was bad, and I am mad at you!" As she signed the words she stressed them, making sure the little girl understood. "Do you know why I am mad at you?" she asked.

Jennifer nodded her head and began to sob with shame.

Lauri made her look at her. "I'm going to spank you so you'll remember next time not to bother someone else's things. Do you want me to mess up your room? Do you want me to break your toys?"

Jennifer shook her head.

Lauri led her over to the commode, sat down on it, and bent the child over her knees. She swatted her bottom three times with the palm of her hand. Jennifer was crying in earnest now.

"What in the hell do you think you're doing?" Drake demanded from the doorway.

Lauri raised Jennifer up and tried to hug her, but the child ran out of her arms and into the sympathetic embrace of her father, who was glaring at Lauri.

She said calmly, "I should think that would be readily apparent. I'm giving Jennifer a well-deserved spanking."

"Don't ever spank her again," he commanded curtly as he continued to pat the child's back. She sobbed into his shoulder.

"I certainly will, and I'll thank you not to come along and rescue her when I do."

"She can't understand why you're spanking her."

"Of course she can!" Lauri protested, now growing angry. "Do you think I'd let her get by with something like this without punishment? Where would it stop?"

He had returned Jennifer to her feet and stood facing Lauri with his hands on his hips. "What are you? Some kind of sadist? Do you get your kicks from beating up on little handicapped kids?"

Lauri had never been so livid in her life and she felt the heat of fury filling her body even as her face drained of all color. "You pompous ass," she hissed through clenched teeth. "How dare you accuse me of such a thing." She took a step forward with her hand drawn back, fully intending to slap him. "How dare—"

She was diverted by Jennifer, who was tugging on Lauri's jean leg. "Auwy," she pleaded. Lauri glanced down and saw that Jennifer was holding up a tube of lipstick that had been wiped clean and whose cap had been replaced. The child signed *I'm sorry*.

Lauri forgot Jennifer's father and knelt down to hug the little girl to her. She brushed back the tangled curls from the tear-streaked face. "I'm sorry it happened too. Will you help me clean it up?" she asked, and Jennifer nodded eagerly and began by picking up the discarded, soiled tissues that littered the carpet.

Lauri stood up and faced Drake squarely, ready to resume her tirade, but his face had changed. He wasn't challenging her. He wasn't angry. He was watching his daughter. Slowly he raised his eyes to Lauri.

They communicated something she couldn't decipher. She read in the green depths a glimmer of understanding. He knew her purpose, and had more or less recognized her objectives. Total comprehension was beyond him, however, and he searched her face, her eyes, for that element that eluded his grasp.

Too soon, he seemed embarrassed by this uncommon susceptibility. She saw the veil slip over his eyes before he hurriedly looked away. "I'll leave you ladies alone," he murmured as he left the room.

Chapter Seven

❦

For the next several days there were no major upheavals. Lauri continued to conduct Jennifer's lessons in the mornings while Drake conveniently made himself scarce.

Lauri was glad to see that the tired lines around his eyes were gradually fading, and he seemed more relaxed than when he had arrived. He no longer wore the European cut coats and monogrammed shirts. Instead, his uniform was a pair of faded jeans that did nothing to hide, but rather enhanced, his virility. Western shirts and cowboy boots acclimated him into the mountain village like one of the natives.

He teased her and prodded her with innuendos, but made no more overt advances. She told herself she was relieved. But sometimes she resented his ability to disregard her while she was increasingly aware of him.

Late one morning Betty volunteered to take Jennifer and her two children on a picnic. Lauri was thankful for the break and knew that Jennifer would enjoy an outing. Without a moment's hesitation she put Jennifer in Betty's care.

A walk through the woods may not be such a bad idea, Lauri mused as she nibbled on a sandwich for lunch. The autumn weather was bracing, and the aspen trees were in their full golden glory. She decided to take advantage of the day.

As she passed the laundry room on her way out, she heard Drake whistling softly. She stuck her head in the door to tell him she was leaving but stared in astonishment when she saw what he was doing.

"What do you think you're doing?" she gasped.

At the sound of her voice, he turned around and grinned a greeting. "Hi. Where's Jennifer?"

"She's gone on a picnic with Betty," she answered absently. Then pulled herself upright and asked again with biting tones. "What do you think you're doing?" He was holding one of her sheer, glossy brassieres in his hand.

"What does it look like I'm doing?" he asked sarcastically, enunciating each word. "I'm sorting the laundry. This is a democratic household. I intend to do my share of the labor." He held up the bra by the straps and studied it with a knit brow.

"But—put down— Those are my—" She was so

undone by his handling her intimate apparel that she couldn't complete a thought.

"Well, I didn't think they were Jennifer's," he scoffed. "And I knew damn well they weren't mine." He studied the label on the garment. "'Dusty rose.' Now why didn't they just name it pink? And these," he reached for a pair of sheer, scanty panties, "are 'daffodil.' Why not just yellow? It's easier to spell."

"Will you please stop fondling my underwear like some pervert!" she cried. "I will wash my own things."

"Don't worry, Lauri," he said with irritating condescension. "I know not to wash them in the machine. I even know to wash them in cold water with a mild detergent. Have you forgotten that I'm on a soap opera? I didn't stay with that show for seven years without learning something!" He was making fun of her, and she stamped her foot in irritation.

"Drake—" she ground out threateningly.

He was looking at the tag on the bra again. "Thirty-four B. That's not very big, is it?" he asked. His eyes rested on her breasts and appraised them clinically. If he had actually touched her, she couldn't have felt the impact any stronger. "But then," he continued objectively, "I guess you'd look funny with great big ones. You'd probably fall over from having to carry them around."

He was talking in a detached voice, but the light in his eyes belied his disinterest. "Let's see," he said, and tossed the lingerie on the washing machine.

Before she could guess his purpose, he came to her and closed his eyes. By feel his hands accurately found her breasts and closed over them. His palms made lazy, slow circles over her. He caressed her tenderly, pressing his fingers into her softness. When he felt the expected reaction under the maddening teasing of his thumbs, he opened one eye and looked down at her.

"Just as I thought," he whispered. "A perfect thirty-four B." His lips melded into hers in a kiss that promised as much as it fulfilled. Her lips were open and ready for him, matching his ardor with equal passion. His hands left her breasts, and his arms encircled her and drew her against him in an encompassing embrace.

The muscles of his thighs strained through the denim of his jeans and pressed into hers as she arched against him. Her spine was explored by an inquisitive hand before it settled on the curve of her hip and imprisoned her next to his hard strength.

Her hands went around his neck and pulled his head down to her. She turned her face with an abandoned movement so that her features were caressed by the silky mustache. It brushed her chin, her lips, her nose. It feathered her cheekbones and flirted with her eyelids.

He indulged her play until his hunger for her overcame generosity. He captured her mouth and plundered it with his tongue. The silver-brown strands of his hair were pulled through her fingers, which tingled with nerve endings newly born.

"Lauri, you can't imagine what torture this is for me,"

he grated when he lifted his mouth from hers and settled it against her ear. To clarify his meaning Drake cupped her jean-clad bottom in his hands and ground his hips against her.

A thrill of desire knifed through her that was so startling, she was suddenly fearful of her own response. Drake, she knew, was beyond reasoning, but one of them had to remain sane. Were this to continue, she might realize fulfillment of her longing for him, but the price would be too high. She couldn't let it happen.

"Drake," she said with a sob, "we mustn't."

His breathing was uneven as he rasped in her ear, "Yes, we must. If we don't, I'm going to explode."

"Drake, please," she said desperately, and tried to push him away. "No, no," she pleaded, for she was still in danger of returning to that plane of oblivion where passion colored all rational thought.

He raised his head and glared down at her. The hands gripping her upper arms were like steel bands. "Why? Dammit, why?" He shook her slightly. "Do you get some kinky thrill from doing this to me?" He thrust his hips against her again.

She swallowed hard in embarrassment and diverted her eyes from his penetrating gaze. She had felt the unmistakable power of his desire, and it had quickened her senses with a renewed longing. She wanted to say, "If you loved me, I would make love to you in an instant. But I can't be a substitute for a ghost. I can't be hurt again by someone who needs me only when the mood

117

strikes him." She couldn't say any of that. Even if she did, it would make no difference; they would still be at square one. He would still love Susan's memory.

"Drake, you know it's not wise for us to play with fire this way. If we became involved, I would have to leave Jennifer. I'm living with you, but only in the sense that we're sharing an address. Paul tried to talk me into living with him before we were married. I couldn't do it then. I can't now. It's old-fashioned, I know, but that's how I was brought up."

"Yeah?" he slurred. "Well I've been brought up frequently of late, and have nothing to show for it but an ache in my loins."

She gasped at his crudity. "That's disgusting," she spat. "Let me go!"

Roughly he shoved her away from him as he took a step backward. To their common surprise she went with him and barged into his chest. His arms went around her for support.

"What—" she started to ask as Drake bellowed with laughter.

"I don't know to whom this retribution belongs, but it appears that we're welded together."

"What?" she asked incredulously.

"Our belt buckles are hooked together," he explained.

She glanced down at her waist and saw that he was right. His jeans were belted with a large, ornate buckle on a western leather belt. She had on jeans, too, and though her buckle wasn't western like his, somehow the metal of the two had become enmeshed during their embrace.

She looked up at him in shock. "What do we do?" she asked.

He was amused by their predicament. "We can have a helluva lot of fun." He paused when her eyes opened wide in alarm. "Or we can try to get them undone," he added smoothly. "In either case I can't see what I'm doing. Move your torso to the left a little so I can see."

When her breasts raked across his chest as she did as he directed, she jerked her head up to see if he had noticed, and his delighted, silly grin confirmed that he had. "See how much fun this is?" he mocked.

"Will you please hurry," she admonished. "What would happen if the house caught on fire?"

"We'd give the firemen something to talk about for years to come."

"Drake—"

"Okay, okay, party pooper." He studied the metal buckles as well as he could from his angle. "Slip your hand into the waistband of my jeans," he said at last.

Lauri looked up at him skeptically. "Oh, sure," she said dryly.

He couldn't help but break into a big grin. "I'm not kidding. Slide your hand behind my buckle, and when I say so, push out on it."

She sighed and eyed him warily as she tentatively slipped her hand into the tight jeans. His shirttail was parted under the waistband, and her hand encountered warm skin covered with satiny hair. Inadvertently her eyes trailed to the neck of his shirt, where the dark curls were crisp and crinkly. The contrast was electrifying. Instinctively her fingers moved under the tight jeans to investigate further.

His eyes darkened for an instant, and a muscle in his jaw twitched, but he looked down quickly to the trapped buckles. "Now I do this," he said as he slid his hand into Lauri's waistband. She gasped and sucked in her breath in reaction, creating a hollow in her stomach and succeeding only in giving his hand more freedom.

"I'm only doing what's necessary," he said sanctimoniously. But his fingers stirred against the smooth skin of her abdomen, and Lauri could feel her pulse pounding through her veins.

"Move your head to the left again," he said near her head. His breath fanned the tendrils of auburn hair on her temple. In response to the curious fingers under her jeans, her breasts pressed hard and pointed against his chest. She couldn't raise her eyes to look at him.

"Okay . . . now push out on my buckle," he said. She did as she was told while his fingers worked from her side. In a few seconds there was a sound of grating metal and then the buckles snapped apart.

Lauri quickly withdrew her hand. Drake's hand abandoned the warmth inside her jeans much more slowly, but she stepped away from him immediately.

Placing her hands on her hips, she demanded, "What

was so difficult? Why couldn't I have pushed my own buckle at the same time you did yours?"

He shrugged nonchalantly and leaned against the washing machine. "I guess you could have, but elbows would have been sticking out all over the place, and I probably couldn't've seen what I was doing." His eyes began to twinkle. "And it wouldn't have been nearly as stimulating."

"You—you—" she stammered, stamping her foot and shoving him out of the way to retrieve her frilly underwear. "From now on I'll do my own laundry, thank you!"

As she stormed out of the laundry room his laughter followed her.

"I'll get it," Lauri called as she crossed the living room to answer the front-door bell. She had left Drake in the kitchen to do the breakfast dishes when she and Jennifer went into the classroom to begin lessons.

It was three days since the scene in the laundry room, but any recollection of it precipitated shallow breathing and a rapid heartbeat, which were annoying. Lauri had studiously avoided Drake whenever possible. Much to her irritation he regarded her avoidance as highly amusing.

He stalked her. He watched every movement and calculated her reactions to any given situation. In defense she showed him her temper often, but he only grinned sardonically, provoking her further.

She opened the front door and greeted the large bearded man standing on the other side of the threshold. "John! Come in."

"Thank you, Lauri. I hope I'm not interrupting anything."

"No. Jennifer and I are about to start her lessons, but they can wait. She'll want to see you. You're one of her favorite people, you know." Lauri smiled up at the man whom she had privately tagged "the gentle giant."

One afternoon she and Jennifer had been strolling the hilly streets of Whispers and were attracted to a woodcrafts shop. The proprietor was John Meadows. He was an enormous man with wide shoulders and a massive chest that tapered into legs that were as large as tree trunks. His dark brown hair hung almost to his shoulders and blended into a luxuriant beard. Sad brown eyes looked out at the world from under shaggy brows.

Incongruous with his size, which could have been intimidating, was his soft-spoken, gentle, and kind disposition. He had been immediately enchanted by the red-haired young woman who walked into his shop holding the hand of an angelic-looking child.

The shop was small and cluttered and smelled pungently of wood and varnish. John made furniture as well as beautiful wood carvings. His large hairy hands handled the intricate tools of his trade like a master.

Lauri had been delighted when he spoke in sign to Jennifer, and the three had developed a fast friendship.

Several days a week, when Lauri had an errand in town, she and Jennifer would visit John while he worked.

Jennifer bounded out of the classroom with unrestrained joy after Lauri informed her of their guest. She ran to John, who leaned down and lifted the little girl high over his head with his brawny arms. She squealed in delight.

Her high laughter brought Drake out of the kitchen. He stared curiously with narrowed eyes at the overall-clad man who was holding his daughter with such familiarity.

I've brought you a present, Jennifer, John signed as he returned her to the floor and knelt down on one knee beside her. He reached into the deep pockets of his overalls and pulled out a tissue-wrapped box.

Jennifer took it shyly and looked toward Lauri for direction and approval.

"What do you say to John, Jennifer?" Lauri asked.

Thank you, Jennifer signed.

John returned a *You're welcome*.

"Go ahead and open it," Lauri instructed when Jennifer only played with the red ribbon tied around the package. Jennifer giggled as the indulgent adults looked on. She tore the ribbon and paper off the box and lifted the lid. Inside were three figurines representing a family of bears. Jennifer made a small *ooooh* sound as she reverently lifted the carved wooden pieces out of the box.

"I thought you might use them in coordination with a story. There's a papa bear, mama bear, and baby bear," John said with his gentle smile and soft voice.

"Oh, John, they're lovely," Lauri remarked, bending down to inspect the figures. "I certainly can use them, and I add my thanks along with Jennifer's. She'll treasure them for a long time, I'm sure."

"I don't believe I've had the pleasure," Drake cut in with a voice twinged with sarcasm.

He walked up to John and extended his hand. "Drake Rivington, Jennifer's father."

Was it Lauri's imagination, or had he stressed his relationship to his daughter?

"I'm sorry, Drake. I didn't see you or I would have introduced you," Lauri said. "This is Jennifer's and my friend John Meadows. He's a wood craftsman and has a delightful shop here in Whispers. Jennifer and I made his acquaintance the first week we were here, and have enjoyed visiting him ever since."

"Hello, Mr. Rivington." John's hand surrounded and obscured Drake's. "It's a pleasure to meet you. You have a beautiful child. I've enjoyed her company, not to mention Lauri's." His brown eyes alighted on Lauri with obvious warmth. Neither he nor Lauri saw the twitch in Drake's jaw and the flash of anger that flickered in his green eyes.

"How long have you lived in Whispers?" Drake asked.

John returned his attention to Drake and faced him politely. "Ever since I left college. About eight years ago."

124

"How many years were you in college? You no doubt obtained several degrees." Lauri was stunned by Drake's rudeness. He was deliberately baiting John, and she couldn't understand why. She glared at him in irritation, but he was staring at John and ignoring her.

John didn't seem bothered by Drake's hostility and answered pleasantly, "I only have one degree, in philosophy."

"Hmm," said Drake, leaving the unmistakable notion that he meant, "That figures."

Lauri was furious with him, but controlled the anger in her voice as she asked John, "Would you like to sit down and have a cup of coffee?"

"No, I have to get back and open up the shop. I'm an hour late as it is, but I wanted to get these over to Jennifer." He glanced down at the child, who was sitting on the floor with her family of bears and chattering to them, unaffected by the tension between the three adults. "I also needed to tell you that I can't make our standing date this Tuesday night. I have to go to Santa Fe and pick up some supplies. I may be there for several days."

Out of the corner of her eye Lauri saw Drake pull himself up straighter and cross his arms over his chest in a gesture of annoyance.

"That's all right, John. We'll come down to see you when you get back."

"Good." He smiled gently at her and then turned to Drake. "It was nice to meet you, Mr. Rivington. Please come down to the shop sometime."

"I doubt that the occasion will ever arise, but I'll keep it in mind." He looked at Lauri slyly before he added, "Now that I'm living here, I doubt that Lauri and Jennifer will be seeing you as often. I plan to keep them busy."

Lauri was suffused with anger and abashment. His implication was clear, and John hadn't missed it. He looked down at her with a quizzical expression. Then the shaggy brows smoothed placidly over his brown eyes. They reflected only understanding and were without censure. Lauri wanted to hug him for his innate kindness and tolerance.

He knelt down to Jennifer's level and they communicated several sentences. Lauri tried to get Drake's attention, but he purposely kept his eyes away from her as he examined his thumbnail with absorbing thoroughness.

"I'm sorry I've kept you from your schedule, Lauri," John said as he stood up, towering over her. "I hope I'll see you soon."

"Thank you again for stopping by and bringing Jennifer the gift. Come back anytime," she said sincerely.

John cast a wary eye toward Drake, but he only nodded and said succinctly, "Mr. Meadows," and didn't second Lauri's invitation to John.

John returned Drake's nod, said, "Lauri," then stepped through the door and lumbered down the steps from the porch.

Lauri shut the door softly, controlling the impulse to slam it with the fuming anger she wanted to direct toward

Drake. She turned around slowly to face him. He was waiting for her with both hands on his hips.

She was seething, and her voice quivered when she said, "You were unspeakably, unreasonably rude to that nice, considerate man, and I want to know why."

"And I want to know why you have been dragging my daughter around with some middle-aged hippie."

"Hippie!" she cried furiously. "What history book did you find that in?"

"He's right out of the sixties, for God's sake. Dirty, hairy. It's a wonder he wasn't wearing ropes of beads around his neck. And his name *would* be John. The Beloved," he ridiculed. "His type can't make it in the real world, so they become professional students or hibernate in mountain towns and call themselves artisans. He looks like a yeti. Or Grizzly Adams."

"*You* wear a mustache, Mr. Rivington," she stressed.

"Mine doesn't have flecks of Crest toothpaste in it either," he shouted back at her.

"You just said he was dirty! Make up your mind."

He glared at her dangerously and crossed to her in two long strides. He gripped her upper arms and pulled her to him. "What is this standing date every Tuesday night, huh? Do you take Jennifer along on that too?"

She extricated herself from his grasp and shoved away from him. "Yes, we do. Each Tuesday night John keeps his shop open an hour later. We meet him when he closes and go to dinner."

"I'm sure, being the *nice, considerate man* he is," Drake sneered, "that he brings you home. How long does he stay? Does he open his little shop an hour later the next morning?" His voice dripped with sweetness though his face was set in rigid lines. What he was suggesting was so ridiculous that, had Lauri not been so angry, she would have laughed at him.

"That's none of your damn business," she lashed out.

"Like hell it isn't. This is my house!"

"Not everyone is ruled by their baser instincts—as you are, Mr. Rivington," she accused scathingly.

"I'll show you my baser instincts," he growled. "I've been wanting to for a long time." He captured her again, and this time there was no escaping. His arms pinioned hers to the sides of her body. Efforts to break his hold would be futile, but Lauri refused him the kiss he sought. She clamped her lips and teeth together, denying the inclination to relax them beneath his crushing mouth.

After long moments he raised his head. She had her eyes squeezed tightly shut, but curiosity got the best of her, and she opened them to slits. His face hovered over hers. "You're afraid to kiss me, aren't you? You know what happens to you each time you do, and you fight it, don't you?"

She couldn't believe his audacity and conceit. "No!" she exclaimed. He smiled lazily and dropped his arms.

"Then prove it," he taunted. "Kiss me and convince me that it doesn't make you tingle all over." His eyes were challenging as they raked over her, pausing at the places he knew would react to his kiss.

Had he tried to force her to kiss him, she could have resisted. But it was that mocking dare that struck a chord. She couldn't walk away from it. Her temper had reached a boiling point. Obviously she couldn't fight him physically and win, but she could get the better of him some other way. She would show him that she didn't succumb to his charm like every other woman he met. She'd show him that she wasn't susceptible to his sexuality.

Her eyes narrowed and resembled glowing coals as she raised her arms and cradled his head between her palms. She hesitated a moment, but when he cocked an eyebrow in a questioning arch, she continued with strengthened resolve. This was still a game to him.

She touched his lips lightly with hers. He didn't respond, surrendering all initiative to her. She nibbled at the corners of his lips just under the mustache. She felt his slight shiver, which goaded her on. She was getting to him.

Her tongue outlined his lips until they finally parted. Before reason or common sense could deter her, she thrust her pink tongue between his teeth. She assured herself that it was only a conditioned response and not an electric thrill of shock that made her hands clasp his head more tightly and bring it down closer to hers. It was only a physical reaction and not an emotional necessity that brought her body against his till her breasts were flattened against his broad chest.

She moved her head and searched his mouth with her darting tongue, tasting the essence of him and savoring the flavor. Still he hadn't brought his arms around her. He was acquiescent, but nonparticipating.

Lauri's senses were reeling. She had accepted his dare but was fighting not to become the victim of her own strategy. Thus far she hadn't broken him. It was *her* blood that was racing; his head wasn't pounding with the tempo and vibrancy of a drum's. A throbbing heaviness in the center of her body evidenced all too clearly that she was a woman responding to a man.

She couldn't let him know. She must bring him to a response and conceal her own. The cause would forever be lost if she didn't win this battle.

Her lips continued to tease his mouth, before moving to his chin and neck. Her hand shyly slipped down and investigated the triangle at the base of his throat. Curiously she explored the crisp hair on his chest. Putting down all self-consciousness and averring that her actions were generated by a will to win—and not a deep longing to touch him—she slipped her hand inside his shirt and smoothed her fingers over the muscles under that mat of dark hair.

His breath quickened, and she heard a faint hiss of anguish. Good! she thought. It's working. Not believing her temerity, she trailed her lips to that hollow in his neck that her fingers knew well and explored it leisurely with her mouth. Her hand found the hard, brown button of flesh nestled in the curling hair on his chest and worried it with playful fingers.

A low animal moan was emitted from his throat a heartbeat before his arms came around her and crushed her to him with a ferocity that was staggering. Her arms twined around his neck as his mouth fastened on hers. Their bodies molded together.

His tongue plunged into her mouth and claimed ownership, banishing any objections that might suggest otherwise. Gone was the need to prove indifference. Lauri knew the game was over, and she was willing to admit defeat if Drake would continue kissing her this way. She would gladly suffocate under his heavenly assault.

It was Jennifer who brought them back to reality. She had been playing with her new toys from John when she noticed that her daddy and Lauri were kissing. She stood up and tugged on Drake's pant leg, vying for attention and wanting to join this fun new game.

He pulled away from Lauri and stared at her for long moments. His eyes were clouded with desire, and she realized then that the victory belonged to neither of them. He had been as disturbed and aroused by her kiss as she had come to be by his.

Jennifer refused to be ignored and made a stronger protest over being neglected. Drake tore his gaze from Lauri and reached down to pick up the offended child.

"Who is this? Who is this that keeps pestering me, huh?" Drake asked playfully, and tickled Jennifer on the stomach. She reached one chubby arm around his neck and the other around Lauri's and brought all three heads together for a smacking kiss. She let out a peal of laughter and then pulled them all together again. This kissing ceremony was repeated several times until they were all laughing.

"I think school's out for today, don't you?" Drake asked Lauri over Jennifer's blond curls. "That car is costing me money to leave it parked outside. Why don't we drive into Albuquerque and turn it in at the car-rental office? We'll eat dinner somewhere and drive back. Do you think Jennifer can stand the trip?"

"Sure. She needs the break anyway. What should I wear?" She asked because she didn't know if she should go in jeans and expect hamburgers for dinner or dress up in preparation for some fancier restaurant.

His eyes traveled down her body and back up again. "I couldn't care less," he drawled. His eyes said that he'd just as soon she didn't wear anything.

Despite the passion she had displayed only moments before, Lauri blushed hotly and gathered Jennifer in her own arms. "We'll be ready in half an hour," she said quickly, and hastened upstairs.

Chapter Eight

❦

The day turned into a pleasant diversion for them all. Jennifer rode with Drake in the rental car while Lauri followed them in the Mercedes.

She was grateful for the solitude. She had time to sort out her turbulent thoughts. It was dangerous for her and Drake to kiss as they had done earlier in the day. She had told him they shouldn't play with fire, yet they continued to do so.

A thousand times she reassured herself that nothing more would come of it than harmless kissing. But the kissing wasn't harmless, and she knew it. She honestly didn't know how long she could hold Drake at bay or if she wanted to. Should they have an affair, it would mean she couldn't continue teaching Jennifer. That would be a grievous situation for all of them, especially the child. She would be the innocent victim of the behavior of two adults who should know better than to jeopardize her future this way.

In the quiet privacy of the Mercedes that glided over the mountain roads toward the city, it was easy for her to vow never to be drawn again into the circle of Drake's arms. With determination she could resist the persuasion of his hands and lips. It was only a matter of discipline, and Lauri Parrish had always prided herself in possessing that virtue.

She'd not let Drake touch her again. Her decision was made.

And it meant absolutely nothing.

The moment they arrived at their destination, he walked up to the car and helped her alight. His extended hand was accepted without hesitation, and she brushed against him as they walked, anxious to feel the hard, lean strength of his body next to hers.

The matter of the car was settled with dispatch. They did some shopping in Albuquerque's most exclusive stores. Drake bought Jennifer a bright blue ski jacket, which Lauri said was outlandishly expensive. He only shrugged off her objections. Jennifer wanted to wear it home, but though it was a chilly autumn day, Lauri explained that the new coat would be much too warm. The child conceded to have it packed in a box when Drake bought her a cardigan sweater with a fur-trimmed hood.

As usual, the salesladies were flustered and clumsily

overattentive while waiting on them. Customers in the store stopped their own shopping to stare in a way that made Lauri terribly self-conscious.

Several of the women glared at her in open envy. Their expressions were full of speculation and hostility. Drake didn't help her uneasiness. He constantly asked her opinion and treated her with a familiarity that was indicting.

Lauri felt immense gratification for one thing: Drake spoke in sign to Jennifer without embarrassment or apology. He seemed totally unaffected by his fans seeing him with his handicapped daughter.

Lauri had compromised; her outfit was neither too casual nor too dressy. She had worn a light brown wool skirt and a jade silk blouse. When they got out of the car to go into the restaurant, she decided it was cool enough to put on her off-white wool blazer.

Drake held it for her as she slipped it on, and he kept a proprietary arm around her shoulders as they walked into the restaurant. Lauri thought they made an attractive family unit as the maître d' seated them, then immediately chided herself for the fanciful thought. She knew what Drake's feelings were; he had made his intentions clear. He would enjoy a physical relationship, but his heart would always belong to Susan.

On the drive home Jennifer became sleepy and rested her head on Lauri's lap. Bunny, her constant companion, had been brought along, and he was snuggled under her arm.

Drake reached toward the radio dial and found a soothing FM station. His hand came back to rest on Jennifer's soft curls, and he patted her head for several minutes until he knew she was in a sound sleep.

Lauri had expected him to return his hand to the steering wheel, and her heart lurched when he settled his hand on her thigh, behind Jennifer's head. He squeezed Lauri gently. She looked at the twilight-soft scenery outside, at the lighted dashboard of the car, at the sleeping child in her lap—anywhere but at the man beside her.

Of their own volition her eyes traversed the interior of the car and looked at Drake's perfect profile. He seemed to sense her eyes on him and turned his head to meet her gaze. He saw the warmth that radiated from her amber eyes and smiled tenderly.

His hand moved up her thigh and touched her with an intimacy that melted resolutions and obliterated caution. His hand remained where it was until the lights of Whispers came into view, and he had to place both hands on the steering wheel to negotiate safely the curving, hilly streets.

They had no trouble getting Jennifer to go to bed. She drowsily submitted while Lauri undressed her and tucked her into bed. After the ritual of prayers and kisses Drake turned out the light in her room.

"Would you enjoy a fire in the fireplace tonight?" he asked as they stood in the hallway.

"That sounds very nice. I could stand to unwind for a while before I go to bed. It's been a long day."

"Anything I can do to help you relax?" he asked with an insinuating grin.

"You're incorrigible," Lauri scolded, but she was smiling. "I'm going to take a bath and then I'll join you downstairs."

"By that time I'll have a roaring fire going. I was a Boy Scout, you know."

"You? Impossible!" she said teasingly just before she shut the door to the bedroom and robbed him of an opportunity to retort.

After her bath Lauri wrapped herself in a warm flannel robe and knotted the belt at her waist. The peach color was flattering to her hair and complexion, and the satin lapels added a luster to the skin on her throat.

Living with Drake for the past few days had rid her of some of her initial modesty. She no longer skittered around seeking cover if he should catch her in her robe or without makeup. A certain degree of familiarity had developed between them. Quite unselfconsciously she went downstairs, pulling a hairbrush through the auburn strands still damp from her bath.

She crossed the living room and drew the drapes. Automatically reaching for the lamp, she was halted by Drake's voice. "Can we leave the lights off? The firelight is enough."

He was coming from the kitchen, carrying two wine-glasses and a bottle of white wine in a cooler. The haunting melody of a ballad sung by Johnny Mathis was emanating from the stereo system in the bookcase. True to his word, Drake had a cheerful fire burning brightly.

"It *is* relaxing this way," Lauri said nervously. Relaxing and seductive, she thought warily. Drake had changed out of his slacks and sport coat and put on a pair of old faded jeans and a white turtleneck sweater.

Lauri curled up in one corner of the sofa facing the fireplace. Drake sat the wine cooler and the two glasses on the coffee table in front of her.

"Will you drink *one* glass of wine with me?" he asked as he sat down beside her.

"I—"

"Please. One glass? It will do you good."

Since he was pouring it anyway, Lauri said, "All right. One glass." Their fingers made brief contact when he handed her the wine. She sipped at it tentatively. He was watching her closely. Diverting her eyes from his unsettling stare, she looked at the fire on the other side of the hearth. "It's a lovely fire, Drake. Thank you for thinking of it."

"My pleasure. Except the exertion of building it has made me too warm to enjoy it. Do you mind?" Before she could respond either positively or negatively, he pulled the white sweater over his head.

She had seen him shirtless many times in the past days, but the sight of his broad, furred chest always made her heart do a strange erratic dance. His chest tapered over the ridges of his ribs to a flat, taut stomach.

The jeans were snapped closed two inches below his navel. Lauri's throat constricted when she saw the distinct shape of his masculinity under the tight, soft fabric of the pants. She took another quick sip of wine.

"You smell good," he said, leaning toward her slightly. He didn't touch her, but brought his face to within a breath of her neck. "What is that?"

"I—It—" Lauri couldn't manage the words. She swallowed and tried again. "It's nothing special or expensive. I buy it at the drugstore."

"No apology is necessary, I assure you. It's doing its job."

His words—or was it the nearness of his body?—had an impact on her that she felt to her toes. With a trembling hand she ran the brush through her hair one last time and laid it on the coffee table. Already she could feel the effects of the wine, though she had drunk no more than half her glass. She took one last sip and returned the glass to the table. When she leaned back onto the sofa, Drake had moved much closer to her.

She turned toward him and saw that he was moving his eyes over her hair. "It's beautiful," he whispered. "In the firelight, it's even lovelier than usual." He placed his hand on the top of her head and smoothed it down over the gilded hair to her shoulders.

The firelight cast deep shadows on his features. His eyes were almost obscured under the thick brows, but Lauri knew that they were searching her face. She could imagine that they had touched her when she felt them lingering on her mouth. Drake dipped his index finger in his wineglass and brought it to her lips. He painted her mouth with the golden liquid, moving slowly over her upper lip then the lower one. Under the gentle pressure of his finger, they opened.

He lowered his head and took her lips under his, sipping at the wine, then melding his mouth to hers in a heart-stopping kiss that left her shaky and breathless.

"You're more delicious than the wine. And twice as intoxicating," Drake breathed when he finally pulled away from her. He set his glass next to hers on the table. She expected him to turn back to her and take her in his arms.

Instead, he lay on his back on the couch, stretched out his full length, and settled his head in her lap. He lifted an unresisting hand, kissed the palm intimately, and pressed it on his stomach, covering it with his own hand.

"This must be Heaven," he said, staring up at her. "The view from here is not to be surpassed." His eyes twinkled as they scanned her breasts, outlined clearly under the clinging fabric of her robe. He laughed when Lauri blushed. Then he sighed deeply, contentedly. "I love this place, don't you, Lauri?" She was surprised at the sudden seriousness in his voice.

"Whispers? Yes, it's wonderful. I'll confess that I thought you'd be well on your way back to New York by now though."

"Sometimes I miss the lights and cameras. I'd be

lying if I said I didn't. But I really dread returning to the life and loves of Doctor Glen Hambrick. I didn't ever really want that job in the first place."

"You didn't?"

The astonishment must have been apparent in her voice because he opened his eyes, which had been closed, and answered. "No, I didn't."

"Then why— How?" she stammered.

"Susan talked me into going to the audition." Lauri reacted instantly when he said his wife's name, but it hadn't seemed to pain him as it had done in the past.

"I was what they were looking for," he continued. "I kissed this actress who at that time was the leading lady on the show. They thought we looked good together. I had the part before I knew it."

"What did you want to do, Drake?"

"I had the usual goal of every serious aspiring actor— to do legitimate theater. More than acting, though, I wanted to direct. However, after a few years in New York, I found out that one has to pay rent, and eat, and things like that," he laughed bitterly. "I had to work when I could, and not attend the classes I needed."

Absently Lauri stroked the silver-brown hair with her fingers. It was so right that his head be resting in her lap and they be enjoying this peaceful interlude. "Where is your home. Drake? Do you have a family?" It was strange that he had never mentioned anything about his background.

"I grew up in Illinois. See, I'm from the Midwest just

like you are." He moved his head to look up at her and the heavy pressure against her thighs sent a thrill of pleasure through her. "My father was a successful insurance man, though we were never rich. He died when I was still in high school. Mother died two years ago. I have a brother who is a defense attorney. I guess in his own way he's an actor too." He chuckled. "After two years in a liberal arts college, I went to New York, graduated from the American Academy of Dramatic Arts, and then started making every audition I could, hoping to find work."

"I've seen *A Chorus Line*. I don't think I could go through something like that too many times and retain my sanity," Lauri commented.

He laughed. "I don't think anyone with any sanity would put themselves through it. It's a devastating experience. I remember when I auditioned for the part of Danny in *Grease*. I was convinced I was perfect for the part. For weeks I walked around in a black leather jacket. I talked rough and dangled a cigarette from my lips. At the audition when they asked me to sing and dance, I humiliated myself. I knew then that musical comedy wasn't ever going to be my bag. But they wouldn't even let me audition for one of the kids in the crowd scenes. They said my hair looked silver under the lights and they didn't need any old men. I promised to dye it black if they'd let me have a walk-on part of any kind. No soap."

He paused for a moment and rubbed his hand across

the back of hers, which was still resting on his bare stomach. "That's where I met Susan—at that audition. She came up to me afterward and said she was glad that I hadn't gotten the part. She would have hated seeing me dye my hair."

The pain in Lauri's chest squeezed with increasing intensity. His voice had dropped in volume as well as pitch. Susan was still a very integral part of him, though she had been dead for three years. Knowing the answer already, but somehow having to verbalize the question, Lauri asked softly, "Was she beautiful?"

"Yes," he said without hesitation, and shut his eyelids like a curtain over the green eyes. "She was a dancer, a serious pupil of ballet. No matter what show she auditioned for, she was too classic in her style to be in the chorus. She always went back to ballet. Finally she got chosen for American Ballet Theatre."

A ballerina! That was worse than Lauri had anticipated. She would have been dainty and feminine and graceful and, as he had said, beautiful.

She had to change the subject. It was suddenly vital that the mood of moments before be restored. "What is your favorite work, Drake? What role would you most like to play?"

"Brick in *Cat on a Hot Tin Roof*, without qualification," he said. "I did him once in acting class. It's a magnificent character. Every relationship in Brick's life is explored in that two and a half hours. With his wife, his father, his mother, his brother, his friend." His voice was becoming excited. "But I'd love to direct it too. Can you imagine drawing out all the nuances of those wonderful characters? God, what a challenge." He was quiet for a moment while he stared into space, as if seeing an imaginary stage with the actors standing in readiness for his direction. Then he glanced up at her and stared for long moments.

Her hair framed her face as she looked down at him. The firelight made it glow and shimmer. Her complexion, still dewy from her bath, was soft and inviting where her robe gaped open at her throat.

"You don't look like a tutor," he said softly.

"You look exactly like an actor," she whispered back.

He raised up slightly and braced himself by placing his arm on the other side of her hip. "Could you be a bit more specific?" he asked. "I mean, Ernest Borgnine is an actor, and Robert Redford is an actor."

She was laughing. "I see your point. Well, let me see," she squinted her eyes as she perused his face and chest. "I'd say you're somewhere in between."

"Oh, yeah?" he teased. "May I audition for the romantic male lead, Ms. Producer? Please? It will be an audition I'll enjoy."

While he was talking, he tugged on the belt of her robe, and it fell away under his fingers. "As you can see I'm already getting into character." His hand slipped inside the robe and cupped her breast. "All I need now is a supporting player," he said as his lips sought hers and found them willing.

The kiss was deep and long. While one hand continued to caress her breast, his other threaded the burnished auburn hair through his fingers. Her arm went around his naked shoulders and smoothed over the hard muscles. The other hand traced each lean rib until it rested on the curve of his waist.

His mouth finally lifted from hers long enough to murmur, "I hoped I'd find nothing but you under this robe." He slid the robe from her shoulder and nipped at the fragrant skin. "When you're warm and pliant and serene like this, there's a maternal quality about you that I need." His lips trailed down her chest to the top curve of her breasts, which he brushed with his mustache. Slipping his arm inside the robe, he drew her closer against him. "Nurture me, Lauri," he grated huskily.

When his mouth closed over the bud of her breast, Lauri clasped his head and arched against him. His tongue played havoc with her, circling, darting, thrusting. He nibbled her with lazy leisure. She moaned deep in her throat when he nuzzled the undersides of her breasts with his nose and mouth only to return to that which he could never get enough of. He suckled her gently, delectably.

She rested her cheek on the top of his head and explored his chest and stomach with a light but eager hand. Timidly she placed it at the waistband of his jeans. He buried his head between her breasts and rotated it in a suppliant gesture of mingled torment and ecstasy.

"Oh, God, yes. Please, Lauri," he rasped in an uneven

voice that was muffled further by the soft flesh under his lips. "Touch me."

She unsnapped the jeans.

The doorbell sounded like cathedral chimes over the sound of their labored breathing, the strains of violin music on the stereo, and the hissing and popping of the flames in the fireplace.

Drake cursed expansively as he struggled into a sitting position and hung his head over his knees. "Who the hell—"

"Maybe they'll go away," Lauri said hopefully.

The ringing bell announced that whoever it was, wasn't giving up. Drake cursed again, but stumbled to his feet and crossed to the alcove, which prevented Lauri from seeing the front door. She was about to remind him that he was shirtless but didn't have time before she heard him open the door.

"Oh! We didn't expect to see *you* here. This is certainly a surprise."

At the sound of the familiar voice Lauri bolted off the couch. Trembling legs almost failed to support her. With useless fingers, she straightened her robe and secured the belt at her waist. "Oh, Lord," she cried silently, and barely stifled a sob.

"Who—" Drake started, only to be interrupted.

"I'm Reverend Andrew Parrish, Lauri's father. Is she here?"

Chapter Nine

❦

"Uh, good evening," Lauri heard Drake say. "I'm—"

"We know who you are, young man. Lauri's told us all about you. Mother has been flittering around like a moth, telling everyone that her daughter works for Drake Sloan."

"I can't believe that I'm talking to you in person. The ladies back home will—"

"Mother, please, can't you see the man is shirtless and we're keeping him out in the night air. May we come in, Mr. Sl—I mean, Mr. Rivington?"

Lauri had listened to this exchange in a state of shock as she stood rooted to the spot in front of the sofa. Her impulse was to run up the stairs and hide, but they were in view of the front door. There was no way she could reach them without her parents seeing her.

What were they doing here? They would think—they would *know*— What could she do? She straightened her robe as well as possible and smoothed an ineffectual hand over her hair, which was helplessly mussed. She had no more time. Drake was escorting her parents into the room.

"Mother! Daddy!" she exclaimed with false enthusiasm and rushed across the room to greet them. She would just have to brazen it out. Don't act guilty, she cautioned herself.

"Lauri, my dear girl. How are you?" Alice Parrish hugged her daughter in a tight embrace, and Lauri knew her mother could feel that she was wearing nothing under her robe. She glanced at Drake over her mother's shoulder. He shrugged helplessly and looked a trifle pale himself. His hair, Lauri noted in anguish, was as mussed as hers. In addition, wearing only his unsnapped jeans, he was announcing his aroused sexuality as blatantly as a flashing neon sign. Oh, God!

Her mother kissed her on the lips, which were abraded from Drake's kisses of moments ago. Could her mother taste Drake on her mouth? She wondered. Then she was being embraced by her father, and Lauri submitted to his hearty hug.

There was an awkward silence when they pulled apart, and her parents surveyed the room. It spelled seduction as if the word had been emblazoned on the walls. The soft music still wafted from the record player, stereo-phonically tempting. The firelight, bathing the room in soft hues and deepening shadows, intimated secrecy. The wine cooler and the half-drunk glasses pointed at them from the coffee table like accusing fingers. Further incriminating were the rumpled cushions of the sofa. One had even been kicked to the floor when Drake had adjusted his long legs on the couch.

Had Lauri not been so mortified by the situation, she would have been glad to see her parents. She had always been close to them and knew she was fortunate to have parents who had shown her nothing but love all her life.

She looked at her mother, who was petite, barely reaching her husband's shoulder. Alice Parrish's hair was the same russet shade as Lauri's, but had faded with age to a less vibrant hue. Her face was virtually unlined, and what creases were there were laugh lines, testimony to her happy disposition.

Andrew Parrish carried his height proudly and with distinction. His dark, gray-streaked hair swept back from his high forehead in well-trimmed waves. He had steady gray eyes that were benign and kind, and spoke with as much spiritual depth as did his deep, reassuring voice. He was a great comfort to his congregation, but he was unswayed in his convictions on morality, no matter how modern the times.

Their initial joy over seeing their younger daughter had been dampened by the scene that now confronted them, and Lauri could read the disillusionment sweeping over those faces that she loved. It broke her heart to see it and know what they must be thinking.

"You met Drake at the door, I believe," she said for lack of anything better and to break the ghastly silence. "What are you doing here? Not that I'm not glad to see you," she added hurriedly. "It's just that I—"

"We thought we'd surprise you, dear. Mother and I are attending a pastors' conference that begins tomorrow night in Santa Fe. We decided to come a day early and spend some time with you."

"I'm delighted you did," Lauri said.

"We didn't expect to find Mr. Rivington here," Andrew said, looking toward Drake. He had picked his sweater off the end of the couch where it had been flung and pulled it over his head.

It was characteristic of her father to get right to the heart of the matter, though Lauri wished she had more time now to come up with a feasible explanation. But would time give her one? She doubted it. Was it her imagination, or was her mother's bottom lip beginning to quiver? Why had they shown up tonight? What if they had arrived fifteen minutes later? Lauri shivered and wrapped her arms around her body. That was too dreadful even to think about.

She licked her lips and said with as much poise as she could conjure, "Drake . . . he came in a few days ago to see Jennifer. Wait till you see Jennifer, Mother," Lauri said shakily. "You'll adore her." When no one said anything, she continued. "He missed her so much, you see. . . . He took time off from the television show. . . . She was so glad to see him. . . ." Laurie trailed off. She wasn't saying anything that made any sense and was skirting the issue she knew was uppermost in everyone's mind.

Andrew eyed the two wineglasses on the coffee table. "He's been staying here with you." She saw the pain in her father's eyes as he said the statement. She wished she could take away that pain. They would never understand. Lauri closed her eyes against the wounded accusation she read on each of her parents' faces.

"Lauri, darling, we may as well tell them," Drake said smoothly, and came to her, putting an affectionate arm around her shoulders and drawing her close. She looked up at him in terror of what he might say. His smile was tender, as he gazed down at her. "I know we agreed to keep it a secret for a while, but when we made that decision, we didn't know that your parents were going to surprise us this way. I'm afraid they're thinking the worst."

And they're right, she wanted to say, but was held mutely spellbound by Drake's words and solicitous manner.

"Sir," he said with formality as he faced her father, "Lauri and I were married today in Albuquerque. You've caught us on our honeymoon."

Lauri would have collapsed to the floor if Drake's arm hadn't supported her. Every ounce of blood in her body rushed to her head, and she could feel each pulsebeat as it pounded through her veins. Her ears were roaring with a cacophony that drowned out her parents' exclamations, though she could see that they were delighted and relieved at the news.

They were laughing and stuttering their astounded congratulations. Her mother came up to Drake and unabashedly embraced him, kissing him on the cheek and saying, "Welcome to our family, Drake." Andrew was thumping him on the back and saying, "You had me going for a minute there. I don't even want to tell you what I was thinking."

Then they were hugging Lauri, and she was swept along in the tide of their love and renewed trust. She was still too stunned to speak or react.

"Andrew, do you realize that we have another grandchild now?" Alice clapped her hands at this exciting thought. "Can we see her, Lauri? I promise not to wake her, but you've told me what a precious child she is. I was so eager to see her anyway, and now she belongs to my family." The lights in Alice's brown eyes were dancing, and Lauri didn't have the heart to disillusion her again.

"She's upstairs, Mother. The smaller bedroom. Why don't you and Daddy go up and see her? I'll put on some coffee. I'm afraid you took me so unawares that my hospitality has been lacking," she said lamely. Her brain could barely form a coherent thought, much less articulate it.

"Come on, Andrew." Alice had her husband by the

hand, and he rolled his eyes heavenward in feigned exasperation. "This woman is crazy about children, Drake. You'll have to get accustomed to her overindulgence."

"I'm looking forward to that, and I know Jennifer will." He spoke warmly. Why wasn't he showing signs of stress? Hadn't he realized that this charade couldn't last? What was his motivation for saying what he had?

As her parents climbed the stairs and disappeared down the hall at the top, she narrowed suspicious eyes on Drake, who gazed at her guilelessly. Her hands balled into fists at her sides. Something in that arrogant tilt of his head sparked her anger. He was enjoying her discomfiture!

"*Why*, Drake?" she demanded in a stage whisper, not wanting her parents to hear this conversation. "Why did you tell them such a ridiculous lie?"

"It was an Academy Award-winning performance, wasn't it? I should think you'd be thanking me for saving your neck, Lauri. The evidence was stacked against you. They were jumping to the correct conclusion, and I don't think you wanted that, did you? And it's a little late for that," he remarked as she switched on the lamp. "You'd do better to leave it off. It's obvious that you've been thoroughly kissed and—"

"Will you stop?" she hissed, and stamped her foot. "Drake, what am I going to do? My parents think I'm married to you! What will we tell them when they discover the truth?"

153

"Tell them that things didn't work out and that we've separated," he said blandly.

She slumped down on the couch and covered her face with her hands. "They were heartbroken when Paul and I separated. I don't want to put them through that again."

He was quiet for a time and then said slowly, "Then I'll tell them that I was only teasing you. You can explain the circumstances of my living here with you. Surely they'll understand. Isn't your father in the business of forgiving?" His bantering voice irritated her more than his bald lie.

"Don't, Drake." Her eyes were fiery, and it wasn't the reflection of the fireplace that caused that dangerous glow. "Don't you dare mock me or them," she warned him in a low, hard voice.

When he saw her cold, forbidding look, he was instantly serious. "I'm sorry. I didn't mean to treat your father's occupation or your predicament lightly."

She could read no insincerity in his face, but she sighed and said with resignation, "It doesn't matter. I'm sure this seems like a scene out of a romantic farce to you, but it's real to me. I couldn't stand to see them hurt."

"Lauri, you're almost thirty years old," he reasoned. "Your life is your own to live as you see fit. They may not like everything you do. No parent does. But they live by their standards and you by yours."

"You don't understand." She groaned. "I've never

done anything to betray their trust. If I chose to do something I knew they wouldn't approve of, I'd keep it from them to protect *them*, not me. I'd never flaunt my indiscretions in their faces."

"But you haven't done anything!" he said sharply, then lowered his voice. "Believe me, I know how chaste you've been. I ache with that knowledge."

In spite of her conflict his words caused her heart to skip a beat. She shifted her eyes away from him. "My conscience is clear, and if I told them the facts of the matter, they'd believe me. It's just that"—she waved her hands as if looking for the right words—"it would make a difference, that's all. They're from a different generation. They'd never accept my living with a man under any circumstances. You've never loved anyone enough to care what they thought of you."

It was the wrong thing to say, and she realized it as soon as the words left her mouth. The planes of his face had gone rigid, and his mouth contorted under his mustache. He crammed his hands in the pockets of his jeans and turned abruptly on his heels to stare into the dying fire.

They heard the Parrishes coming out of Jennifer's room, and Drake said quietly without facing her, "I'll leave it up to you. I'll follow your lead and ad lib."

Alice started talking before she reached the bottom step of the stairs. "Drake, she's an absolute angel. I love her already and can't wait until she wakes up in the morning so I can play with her." Alice's face was radiant with happiness, and it constricted Lauri's heart to continue the deception.

"I'm sorry," she said quickly. "I haven't started the coffee yet." She made a move toward the kitchen, but her father stopped her.

"Don't make any on our account. We're too old to drink it late at night. It keeps us awake. We'd better be finding a place to stay tonight. We'll be back in the morning if that's all right."

"Nonsense," Drake said. "You'll stay here in my house. We have plenty of room."

"Oh, we couldn't," Alice protested. "You and Lauri are on your honeymoon."

"I don't mind, if Lauri doesn't," Drake said with a shrug. "Do you, darling?"

"I—yes. I mean, no, I don't mind," Lauri stammered as she tried to analyze Drake's intentions.

"There's a small bedroom on the other side of the kitchen. That's where I've been sleeping for the past few days. I was going to move into the master bedroom tonight anyway."

"I can understand that," Andrew boomed, and clapped Drake heartily on the back between his shoulder blades. "I, for one, would much rather stay here than a motel. Mother, what do you say?" Andrew asked Alice. Everyone seemed to have forgotten Lauri, who had started violently at Drake's mention of moving into the master bedroom. Now she realized what he had in mind, and it infuriated her.

"Well, naturally I'd rather be here with Lauri," Alice demurred.

"Then it's settled," Drake said firmly. "Let me collect some of my things while Lauri changes the bed. Then we'll let you get some sleep. You must be exhausted."

The next half hour was a concert of confusion. Drake went into the spare bedroom and came back through the living room carrying a box of shaving implements and personal items. A velour robe was draped rakishly over his shoulder. He winked broadly at Lauri as she sat listening to her parents' detailed account of their flight to Albuquerque and the drive to Whispers. She glared at him behind their backs.

She put fresh linens on the bed, working slowly and hoping that Drake would return to the room. She planned to give him a piece of her mind about his sleeping arrangements for the night, but he avoided her. While her parents were saying good night, he put both hands around her waist and possessively drew her back against his chest.

"I'm glad to have you for a son-in-law, Drake. Take care of my daughter and love her. That's all I ask," Andrew said.

"I will, sir," Drake said solemnly. Lauri felt an urge to kick him in the shins.

The older couple retired to their room. Docilely she

followed Drake up the stairs, but as soon as she shut the door to the large bedroom, she faced him belligerently. "I know what you're thinking, Drake, and your little plan isn't going to work."

"What am I thinking?" he asked as he stripped off his sweater for the second time that night.

"You think I'm going to get in that bed with you."

"It never entered my mind," he said offhandedly as he unzipped his jeans.

"What are you doing?" she gulped.

"Taking off my clothes. What does it look like?" As he proceeded to do just that, he said, "I toured with a road company of *Hair* one summer and, since then, have absolutely no modesty. If you're offended, turn around."

His underwear was light blue, tight, and brief, and Lauri swallowed the lump in her throat as he stepped out of the jeans and casually tossed them onto a chair. He turned away from her and began to unfold the covers on the large bed.

"I'm sleeping on the couch," she mumbled as she opened the closet where extra blankets were stored.

"Suit yourself. Your dad may be a minister, but it's obvious that he appreciates the facts of life. What are you going to say to them when they see you there in the morning? Lovers' quarrel?"

She could have slapped his smug face when she turned around and saw him propped up against the pillows, the sheet pulled up to his waist.

"I'll wake up before they do."

"Well, I'm glad you have it all figured out." He yawned and sank down among the pillows. "Good night." .

For lack of a biting reply she stalked out of the room with her arms full of blankets. She crept down the stairs and, with the help of the last flickering firelight, found her way to the bottom.

She jumped in alarm when the overhead light was switched on.

"Oh, dear, I hope I didn't startle you. I was coming up to ask for a few extra blankets," Alice explained. "I'm going to have to sleep on the couch. Your father is snoring so loud, I'll never get any sleep. He does that when he's especially tired, you know. What are you doing with those?" Alice noticed the blankets that Lauri was holding in her arms.

"I—uh—I thought you and Daddy may need them before morning. Even this early in the season, it gets terribly cold here at night." *My mother is sleeping on the couch!* her mind screamed.

"Well I'll be just fine. I may put another log on the fire. Your father wouldn't know if it came a blizzard before morning, so you just get back upstairs to your husband and stop worrying about us." Her mother kissed her on the cheek then turned back into the room. She was wearing the quilted robe Lauri had given her last Christmas. The fragrance of her face cream poignantly reminded Lauri of the moments in her childhood when her mother would come into Ellen's and her room to tuck them in at night.

"Good night, Mother," she said softly as she retreated upstairs.

She paused outside the door of the master bedroom. She considered going into Jennifer's room and sleeping with her, but her bed was not even as large as a twin-size. If she startled Jennifer in the middle of the night, it would raise another ruckus that would need to be explained. She had no choice but to join Drake in the wide bed.

She opened the door quietly and slowly, hoping that maybe he had already drifted to sleep. Her hopes were dashed when he rolled over and looked at her quizzically. She hadn't turned on the light, but moonlight streamed in through the windows, and she could easily see his body outlined under the covers. Her heart thumped painfully against her ribs.

"Having second thoughts?"

"No I'm not," she said with emphasis. "Mother is sleeping on the couch to escape Father's snoring."

"A trait I hope you haven't inherited," he said grouchily as he returned his head to the pillow and faced away from her.

Oh! she fumed silently. He was insufferable. She made as much noise as possible while she brushed her teeth and washed her face. Still harboring her anger, she stripped off her robe and, without thinking, started for the bedroom. What was she doing?! She never slept in nightgowns, but she couldn't climb in bed with Drake like this.

She opened a drawer and took out a pair of panties and a bra and pulled them on. They weren't much, but they were better than nothing—literally. If she wore her robe, she would be sweltering by morning. The lights were out; he would never see her.

She tiptoed to the bed and slid between the sheets, careful to stay on the edge of the bed. She lay her head on the pillow and closed her eyes tightly, commanding her body to relax. She had almost succeeded when his voice came out of the darkness. "Did you put on your suit of armor?"

"Shut up and leave me alone," she threatened, but without much conviction.

"I intend to," Drake said. "For now. But you'll come around." He patted her on the bottom outside the covers before turning over and facing away from her.

Well at least he hadn't forced his attentions on her. She was glad about that. Wasn't she?

A soft violet dawn crept in through the windows. But it wasn't that harbinger of morning that woke Lauri from a deep sleep. She lay on her stomach, her face buried in the pillow. Something warm and moist was caressing her back with slow deliberation. She awoke reluctantly, relishing this euphoric haze between wakefulness and sleep. She wanted this floating sensation to last forever.

The fastener on her bra gave way under skilled fingers, and the thin strap that crossed her back was pushed aside. She awoke fully then, and her muscles tensed under the hypnotic massage that was keeping her in this languorous submission.

"Drake?" she whispered.

"Hmm?" was the only response.

It was hard to conjure up antagonistic feelings while he continued his ministrations. "What are you doing?" she asked breathlessly.

"Having breakfast," he murmured as he nibbled the soft skin on her shoulders. His hands rubbed the small of her back and smoothed over the curve of her hips. "It's delicious."

His voice was no louder than an expulsion of breath. Lauri moaned and pressed her face farther into the pillow when she felt the moist, velvet texture of his tongue sampling the delights of her spine.

One heavy hair-roughened leg was lying across the back of her thighs securing her on the bed while he continued to caress her back with his mouth and hands. He worked his way down to her waist and then started back up. This time he nibbled at her side, along her ribs.

When he reached her armpit, he rolled her over gently onto her back and stared into her slumberous, amber eyes as he stroked the tousled hair away from her face.

"Good morning," he said.

"Good morning."

He slipped the straps of her bra away from her arms,

removing the garment with ease. He looked down at her skin, which was warm and flushed from sleep. Lauri closed her eyes, not able to meet the burning intensity of his gaze as he settled his body over hers.

He raised her arms above her head and, starting at her elbow, kissed and nibbled the sensitive undersides of her upper arms until she wanted to cry out with joy. His mouth trailed across her collarbone and up her neck until he hovered over her lips that were parted and expectant.

His patient arousal of her senses was well rewarded when she kissed him with a fervor that left them both shaken. Tongues, teeth, and lips were choreographed in a beautiful synchronization that brought the dancers to the height of pleasure.

His earlier appetite for her hadn't been appeased, and he was greedy. His mouth and hands begged for cessation of the hunger that had gnawed at him since he had first met her.

"You taste so good. You're sweet . . . warm . . . soft," he whispered as he inched lower and focused his ardent attention on her yearning breasts, which anticipated the relief that only his lips could provide. He set about the welcomed task, and Lauri called his name softly as she grasped his shoulders with her hands.

She forbade any thoughts that might have shadowed the bliss of the moment, but they came unbidden to her mind. Even as she felt the urgency of his desire pressing against her, she was reminded that it was only that—

desire. He didn't—couldn't—love her. When his lust had been gratified, what then? Would he walk away unscathed, leaving her with an empty heart? No! She mustn't let this happen. She could tolerate his arrogance, his role-playing, his scorn, his anger, but she could never withstand his indifference.

Yet, she wanted him. Her mind was denying what her body craved. She arched against his strong length and writhed under the dizzying caress of his mouth on her stomach.

His fingers smoothed over the skin of her abdomen and touched the soft mound that throbbed and felt heavy with moisture and heat. Lauri gasped sharply. His action catapulted her into the realm of reality. Did he even realize it was she who was lying beneath him? Was he thinking of Susan? Imagining—

Lauri's hands were at his shoulders, pushing him away with a strength garnered from panic and revulsion. "No, Drake. Please. No more." He raised his head and saw her anguished face and the tears—which she was unconscious of. They coursed from the outer corners of her eyes till they disappeared in the mussed auburn strands that fanned onto the pillow.

"Lauri?" he asked her softly. He propped himself on one elbow and leaned over her, stopping one rivulet of tears with his finger. The other he sipped from her cheek with solicitous lips.

"I'm not going to ravish you, Lauri," he spoke softly. There was no mocking tone in his voice. "I find that I, too, have a bad case of the scruples. Your folks welcomed me into their family with unconditional acceptance. I wouldn't feel right taking you—as much as I want to—while they're downstairs, believing that we're married." He stroked her temple with his finger and whispered, "You never need to be afraid of me." He kissed her gently on the lips.

She could feel his breath in her own nostrils, in her mouth, when he said, "Please. One more taste of milk and honey." He cupped her breast with his hand and lifted it slightly as he lowered his head. He took the pink crest into his mouth. It was a gesture void of passion, but abundant with longing. He tugged on her gently. It was no more than a flexing of his cheek muscles, but Lauri felt it in every cell of her body.

He disengaged himself from her and left the bed. Stepping into his jeans, he said over his shoulder, "I think I hear Jennifer stirring. I'll get her dressed and meet you downstairs." He paused once more at the door. "For what I gave up this morning, I should either be committed or canonized." He smiled at her tenderly before he left the room.

For a while everything was all right.

165

Chapter Ten

❧

But everything wasn't all right, and there was no reward in pretending it was. Lauri felt like a hypocrite as she sat at the breakfast table with her parents, Drake, and Jennifer. Alice had insisted on preparing a sumptuous breakfast in honor of the newlyweds. For that reason alone Lauri felt guilty.

Alice regaled them with news of Ellen's family, showed them pictures of her two boys, which Drake duly inspected. She told Drake vignettes of Lauri's childhood that made her blush and him laugh. Had she not known better, Lauri would have thought he was enjoying himself. He acted like a new son-in-law striving to impress his bride's family.

He flattered her mother and listened with absorbing

interest when her father launched into one of his stories that were traditionally monotonous. At their urging he divulged the inside gossip surrounding the soap opera. Alice wanted to know about all the behind-the-scenes love affairs—who was married, who wasn't. Was this actress as pretty in person as she was on the show? Did they get to keep the clothes they wore? Who cooked the food they used on the sets? And so on. He answered patiently and even colored some of his tales to make his titillating revelations even more entertaining.

Their conversations were signed for Jennifer's benefit, though everyone knew that she didn't understand it all. Because of Ellen, the Parrishes were accustomed to using sign and used it automatically. Jennifer accepted them immediately, and her acceptance was reciprocated.

If Jennifer had other grandparents, Lauri wasn't aware of it. Drake's parents were dead. She knew so little about Susan, she had no way of knowing if her parents had ever seen their grandchild.

Drake insisted on helping Alice do the breakfast dishes while Lauri made the beds. Andrew settled in the living room to read the newspaper. Jennifer chose to sit on his lap and look at the comics.

Lauri went upstairs to do her morning chores. Unwillingly she acknowledged the lump that rose in her throat, and it took every ounce of will to restrain the tears that pricked her eyelids. This would all be so wonderful if it were true. But it was a sham, a charade. Drake was exercising his acting abilities in a demanding role and performing brilliantly. He should be proud of himself.

Making the large bed that they had shared stirred memories that were plainly etched on her mind. He had been tender and gentle: she had responded to him as she had to no other man in her life.

On her wedding night she had gone to Paul's bed a virgin. Under his impatient guidance her initiation into the rites of love had been less than enchanting, but she had assumed that sex was overrated. Had it lost its mystique through too great expectations? Was the actuality dimmed by eager anticipation?

Vividly she could recall one night when Paul had been particularly disgruntled over a song he was working on. As was his habit when he was frustrated, he came to bed seeking an outlet for his vexation. He had awakened her, and she had sleepily performed the ritual. When his lust had been satisfied, he got up and was pulling on his jeans when he said disgustedly, "You don't trouble yourself to do anything you don't have to, do you?"

She was stung by his words. He had shown no tenderness, no love. There had been no stroking, no attempt to arouse her. Yet he expected her to react with instantaneous passion to his hurried, frantic lovemaking.

By then she was wide-awake, and she sat up in the bed and said heatedly, "I can't turn on like a light switch, Paul, just because you're ready for sex. If you really cared, you'd take a little more time——"

"Don't go coaching me on how to make love!"

"Then coach me!" she cried. "I want to learn to please you. Teach me." She was desperate for his love. Her body and soul cried out for him to love her.

He zipped up his jeans with a gesture of finality. "What good would it do? You'll always be the modest little preacher's kid." He turned away from her and left the bedroom; she had cried herself into an exhausted sleep.

Now, as she smoothed out the bedcovers on Drake's bed, she shivered when she remembered what his touch had been like. He had petted her and caressed her in a way that Paul had never done. He had looked at her body, studied it, praised it, not just used it. She had always dreaded the moment when Paul painfully and abruptly fused his body with hers. For her it had been an invasion, a violation.

Instinctively she knew that it wouldn't be that way with Drake. He would take himself into her as if receiving an esteemed gift. When he had appreciated that gift to the fullest and enriched it by his acceptance, he would return it in a way she had never experienced before.

She thrust those heartrending thoughts from her mind, dressed quickly, and went downstairs. Jennifer wasn't too happy about giving up her place on Andrew's lap and going with Lauri into the classroom. Lauri insisted that they have a few lessons since they hadn't had any the day before when they had played hooky and gone to Albuquerque.

Had that been yesterday?

Andrew made the recalcitrant pupil more cooperative

when he asked permission to join the lessons. Lauri conceded, knowing that her father had participated in Ellen's education and would help her to hold Jennifer's wandering attention.

Drake asked Alice if she would like to see some of the town and she was delighted at his invitation. They left with a promise to return by lunchtime.

If anything, lunch was more festive and relaxed than breakfast. Everyone was having a merry time except Lauri. She was consumed by guilt over this deception, which she made no effort to disclose. It mustn't go on! But how was she to stop it?

Her brows were knit in consternation, and when Drake caught her eye, he had a perplexed expression on his face. *As if you don't know what's wrong with me,* she thought as she threw daggers with her russet eyes.

"Do you ever fish in any of these streams, Drake?" her father asked, interrupting her angry musings.

"Yes, sir. Would you like to fish for a while this afternoon?"

"I didn't bring the proper clothes, although I would have enjoyed that." His voice reflected his disappointment.

"We don't have to be that ambitious about it," Drake laughed. "We can stand on the bank and do some fly casting from there. How about it?" Drake's smile was dazzling, and Lauri was irritated that he could handle this bizarre situation with such aplomb while she was nervous and edgy.

"Why don't you, dear?" her mother suggested. "You'll be cooped up in meetings for the next three days. This mountain air will do you good."

Andrew slid his thumb and index finger down the bridge of his nose while trying to make up his mind. His eyes alighted on Jennifer, and he reached over and patted her curly head. "Only if Jennifer can come with us," he said. *Do you want to go?* he signed.

She turned eager eyes to Lauri. She knew well the word *go*, just as every other child did. *Go where, Lauri?* she asked, as quickly as her chubby hands could move.

Go fishing, Lauri explained, but she could tell by Jennifer's uncomprehending eyes that the gerund had escaped her.

"You come along, Lauri. It'll be a good lesson for her," Drake said.

"No, I need to stay here with Mo—"

"Don't stay on my account," Alice added quickly, interrupting her. "I'm going to work on some needlepoint I brought along, and then I think I'll indulge in a nap. With the telephone ringing at home all the time, I rarely get a chance to have that luxury."

"Then it's all settled," Drake said, standing up. "Come on, Andrew, let's go check out the equipment. It's all stored in that shed out back."

Andrew needed no further invitation, and he hurried after Drake with Jennifer trotting behind them.

"Lauri dear, you'd better go change clothes. I'll do these dishes," Alice said as she began to clear the table.

"Okay," said Lauri dispiritedly. Things were getting out of hand, and she was powerless to do anything about it.

She changed into her oldest jeans, and shoes that mud couldn't damage. She picked up a jacket for Jennifer and one for herself, gathered up several old blankets, and went downstairs. Alice had packed cookies, fruit, and cold drinks as well as a Thermos of coffee in a large bag.

"Mother, we're not going to be gone for more than an hour or so," Lauri protested.

"I know. But you know how hungry one gets when out of doors," she defended.

"You're sure you'll be all right?" Lauri asked.

"Goodness, yes! As a matter of fact, I'll enjoy the privacy. All I'll be doing for the next few days is talking."

The four of them waved good-bye to her as they trekked off in the direction of the foothills behind Drake's lead. He was carrying most of the fishing paraphernalia, but Andrew had insisted on doing his share by lugging the blankets and a tackle box. Jennifer was holding a small creel and Bunny, and Lauri toted the snacks her mother had provided.

It wasn't difficult to find a pleasant spot for their outing. The foothills were ablaze with the golden aspens. The fallen leaves rustled under their feet as they walked through the woods. The brook that Drake had chosen gurgled down from the mountain and sparkled in the sunlight as the crystal-clear water gushed over the smooth rocks lining the stream bed. The sky was an azure bowl turned upside down over the earth; the air was crisp and bracing. All in all it was a perfect autumn day.

The two men set about their fishing, though as Drake had predicted, they weren't too ambitious about it. They derived most of their pleasure simply from casting their lines in the stream and reeling them in. Only a few times did they have a small trout attached to the hook, and these they threw back as soon as Jennifer had cautiously inspected them.

She was a glutton for knowledge. She asked Lauri the names for everything, and her tutor was hard pressed to keep up with her insatiable curiosity. The fishing intrigued her, but when Lauri explained that the fish were usually kept and eaten, her bottom lip began to tremble, and Lauri quickly interested her in the antics of a squirrel who was scampering from tree to tree. They had had a lesson on where food and meat came from, but apparently seeing the animal alive made a difference to the child. They would discuss it some other time when Jennifer was less emotionally involved.

The men joined them for a snack and rested on the blankets that Lauri had had the foresight to bring along. When Drake stood up and walked back toward the stream, Andrew said, "I think I've had enough. Why don't I take Jennifer back to the house, and we'll read a book or do something less strenuous."

"I'll go with you," Lauri said quickly.

"No, no," her father said. "I can find my way, and I

want to spend some time alone with my granddaughter.
You stay here with your husband. I haven't forgotten
that you two are on your honeymoon. I know when to
make myself scarce."

Andrew winked at Drake, who responded with a devil-
ish grin. Lauri had a strong compulsion to slap him.
There was nothing she could do but consent to stay here
alone in the woods with him. She buttoned Jennifer's
sweater with slow deliberateness, prolonging their immi-
nent departure. Andrew was explaining the autumn
leaves to her as they walked off into the trees and left
Lauri with Drake.

"Isn't this cozy?" he asked, scooting closer to her on
the blanket. "Let's wrap up in the blanket."

She pushed him away with the heels of her hands on
his shoulders. "Don't be cute and funny with me. You
can drop your character now. There's no one around to
view your stunning performance of the loving bride-
groom. Please spare me."

"I really bug the hell out of you, don't I?" His face
was far too close to hers. She could see the flecks of
gold and brown in his green eyes.

"Yes, you do!" she flared.

"You'd better be careful," he warned in a singsong
voice and wagged his finger in front of her face. "That's
dangerous."

"What are you talking about?"

He clasped her jaw with strong fingers and forced her
to look at him. He drew her face even closer. In the

merest whisper he said, "If you didn't have the hots for me so bad, I couldn't possibly make you this angry." Before she could retort, he kissed her hard and quick, then hopped to his feet.

She sat there on the blanket and watched as he nonchalantly strolled back to the bank of the stream and picked up the rod and reel. Inwardly she was fuming, but his words had touched a nerve. He was right. Why was she torturing herself? Anger was just one of the emotions he evoked and she displayed them to him far too easily and frequently.

With an elaborate show of indifference she didn't feel, she turned away from him and stretched out on the blanket. Lying on her back. Lauri could feel the sun bathing her face with warmth, and she closed her eyes against its bright rays. He couldn't know that she reveled in remembrances of each kiss, each touch. He couldn't know that her heart pounded whenever she thought about that morning when she had lain naked under his practiced hands and mouth. His hands . . . his mouth . . . his eyes.

She was startled awake when something tickled her ear. She tried to brush it away, but Drake's hand clasped her wrist and held her hand at her chest as he continued to nibble at her ear. His lips moved down her neck, kissing it with brief, elusive kisses that made her light-headed.

He was lying on his stomach, stretched out behind her in the opposite direction so that they formed a straight line with only their heads overlapping. He pulled the collar of her shirt away to allow him unlimited access to her neck. Unconsciously she arched her throat and provided him more room to explore. At last he raised his head and stared down at her.

"Waking you up is becoming a habit-forming pastime. Even upside down, you're gorgeous," he said.

"And you're a liar. I look terrible. I always do when I first wake up."

"Not true," Drake said seductively. "I thought you were gorgeous the first day I saw you standing there looking terrified—but defiant—beside that prop table."

Lauri laughed, remembering. "You were cruel to . . . Lois? Is that her name?" He nodded. "You were cruel to her that day when you said she tasted like an anchovy pizza."

"I never said anything of the sort!" He sounded indignant.

"You certainly did. It took Murray—" She broke off when she saw that he was teasing her. They both laughed. "I can see where it would be difficult to kiss someone you didn't particularly like and make it appear sincere. I'll never understand how actors do that."

"Oh, you learn that in Kissing One-oh-one," he said. "It's a compulsory course in acting school."

"Really?" she asked naively.

"Sure," he replied boastfully. "Here, sit up a minute." She sat up, and they faced each other on the blanket.

"Now," he assumed a professorial voice, "the first

177

kiss you learn is that careless kind given by the negligent or distracted husband. It's usually a near miss. Like this." He demonstrated by kissing the air near her temple. "Or like this," he said, lightly brushing her cheek before quickly turning his head. "It can be used with a little more emotion for welcoming a maiden aunt to the family reunion or greeting a close friend of the family's."

"Is this for real?" she asked dryly.

"Absolutely. We were tested on it."

"A kissing test?"

"I got a perfect score." His teeth gleamed from behind the mustache.

"I'll bet you did."

"Can we get on with the lesson?" he asked in exasperation. She nodded.

"There's the kiss that's hurried and brutal. It's usually motivated by some violent emotion like fear or anger or desperation. It's like this." His fingers bit into the flesh of her upper arms, and she was crushed against him as his lips came down hard on hers.

She was stunned when he pushed her away from him. "See what I mean? The mouth is always closed on that kiss," he said pedantically.

"Thank the Lord for small favors," she mumbled as she tentatively touched her bruised lips.

"The most important kiss, of course, is that of lovers," he continued smoothly. "It takes hours of rehearsal to perfect. It must be convincing. Everyone in the audience must be able to *feel* that kiss.

"Usually the actor takes the girl in his arms like this." He wrapped her in a warm embrace. "Then his lips hover over hers until the audience is panting in anticipation of the actual contact. Then the actor——" He didn't finish because his lips had closed over hers. Into the spirit of the game by now, Lauri raised her arms and encircled his neck. His mouth moved against hers but didn't pursue the kiss any further.

He raised his head and pierced her with his green eyes, which stared directly into hers. His voice was hoarse. "Then there's the kiss that says unequivocably, 'Let's cut this foolishness and get on with it.' It goes something like this."

He leaned against her until she fell back on the blanket under his hard body. His tongue tickled the corners of her lips and outlined the bottom one before it explored the sweet hollows of her mouth. She returned the kiss in kind, teasing and sipping and searching until they pulled apart and gasped for air.

"You're not only an excellent student of kissing, you're a good instructor as well," she said unsteadily.

"Only with the most gifted pupils," he grinned.

She weaved the silver-brown strands of his hair through her fingers. "And how many of those have there been?" she asked jealously.

"Thousands, at least." He traced her lips with a provocative finger. "When she was taking some acting classes, Susan——"

His finger stopped its tender torment, and the name

hung in the air between them, invisible yet puissant. Onto the green eyes that had been liquid and warm spread a steely, cold glaze. For moments that pulsated with tension, they lay perfectly motionless. Then Drake shifted his weight.

"Maybe we should be getting back," he said, rising from her.

She couldn't reply. The constriction in her throat wouldn't permit even the slightest sound. She nodded in agreement.

They gathered up their things in silence. All the sunlight had been extinguished; Lauri felt plunged into gloom. Susan. Always Susan.

They wended their way down the leaf-strewn path toward the house. Drake tried to make conversation, but when he sensed her withdrawn mood, he gave up the effort.

As they approached the house they saw a compact station wagon parked in the driveway. It was parked beside the Mercedes and the Parrishes' rental car.

"Who can that be?" Drake asked as they walked up the sidewalk.

"I don't know. That's not Betty's car."

Drake opened the door and ushered her through. She was met with the lightning flash of a camera. Stunned and momentarily blinded by the bright light, she recoiled and sought the strong support of Drake's chest. Impulsively his arms went around her waist.

"What the hell?" he exclaimed.

The camera flashed again.

"That should be enough for now, son. Let them get in the house at least," Andrew admonished.

When their eyes had adjusted to the dim interior of the house, and the bright purple spots before them had faded to a pale yellow, Lauri and Drake could see the young man who wielded the camera. He was dressed in jeans and jogging shoes, incongruously teamed with a sport jacket, sport shirt, and a necktie.

"Hi, Mr. Sloan. I'm Bob Scott with *The Scoop Sheet*. Boy, this is great!" His permed hair was bouncing like a giant sponge on his head as he bobbed excitedly.

Lauri had no idea why this young man was here in the company of her parents and Jennifer, who was sitting in Andrew's lap and watching the proceedings with avid interest. Lauri was, however, familiar with the publication that Bob Scott named. It was a weekly magazine that was sold by the millions in grocery and convenience stores across the country. It bore lurid headlines that slanted stories, often to the detriment of their subjects. The editors relished uncovered scandals, secrets, and indiscretions. What was he doing here?

As the excited man put the camera to his eye again, Drake dictated, "Will you put that"—he broke off his descriptive word with a swift glance toward Andrew and Alice—"will you put down that camera and kindly tell me what you're doing in my house?"

For the first time some of the exuberance went out of Bob Scott's demeanor. Lauri wasn't surprised. Drake's expression would have intimidated Attila the Hun.

"I—uh—well, sir, I've been tracking you for weeks. There's been all sorts of speculation about why you're not on the set of *The Heart's Answer*. That producer or director or whatever the hell he is—Murray?—well, he wouldn't tell me anything. He's as silent as a corpse. I finally dragged it out of a cameraman that you came here to New Mexico to spend some time with your daughter. I got on your trail—airport, rental car, that kind of thing—and found you here today."

"Well, now that you've found me, what do you want to know?" Drake had learned long ago that these scandal-sheet reporters could be tenacious and that, if one didn't humor them, they could be vicious.

"Well, jeez, you gotta admit that news of your marriage will knock everyone on their ass!" He grinned, but only met Drake's stony stare. Realizing he'd gone too far, he gulped and mumbled, "Excuse me, ladies," addressing Alice and Lauri.

Lauri was incredulous. How could this have happened? Surely Drake would deny their relationship, but then what would she tell her parents?

Alice stood up and came over to Drake, placing a beseeching hand on his arm. "Drake, I hope that you're not upset with me. He came to the house soon after you left. He was talking so fast and asking so many questions that before I knew it, I had blurted out the fact that you and Lauri were married. I know you said you had planned to keep it a secret for a while." Her voice began to quiver. "I'm sorry—"

"Here, now," Drake said moving around Lauri and placing a comforting arm around Alice's shoulders. "I know how reporters can be when they're on the trail of an exclusive story. You've saved me the trouble of having to notify the press myself."

Had Lauri not loved him already, she would have loved him then. He could just as easily have berated her mother, for under that calm facade, she knew he must be furious with the turn of events.

Bob Scott looked somewhat relieved by Drake's more relaxed manner and said, "If I may say so, you sure picked a good-looking chick to marry, Mr. Sloan." He winked at Lauri, who still hadn't culled enough mental fortitude to react to what was happening.

"You may say so, but keep it under wraps," Drake growled, and lowered his brows over his eyes in an exaggerated warning. "I'd like to keep her to myself for a while." He was using his acting skills again. The young, audacious reporter was eating out of his hand now.

"I take it you've met my wife's parents?" Drake asked courteously. Bob Scott nodded. "And this is my daughter, Jennifer." Drake lifted the child up in his arms and patted her back lovingly.

"We all knew you had a little girl somewhere, but you've always steered us away from her. Is that because she's deaf?"

Lauri gasped and expected Drake to grind his balled fist into the reporter's face. Instead, only she saw the muscle in his jaw twitch as he answered smoothly. "No. I wanted to protect her from members of the media who may not be as sensitive as you, Mr. Scott. I didn't put her in a private boarding school because I was ashamed of her."

The reporter licked his lips nervously and said, "Well, jeez, Mr. Sloan. I didn't—I mean—"

"Say hello to Bob," Drake said, interrupting the stammering reporter as he signed the instruction to Jennifer.

Jennifer responded sweetly, smiling that angelic smile that captivated anyone who was graced with it. Bob Scott asked, "How do I say *hi* back?"

Drake showed him, and Jennifer laughed when he awkwardly made the sign. *Go sit by Grandpa*, Drake signed to her as he put her down beside him and patted her on the bottom as she obeyed. When he straightened up, he said, "And this is Lauri. She was Jennifer's teacher." He came to stand beside her and put a possessive arm around her waist, drawing her against him.

"Jeez. Can you tell me how you met?"

Drake embroidered the story outrageously, but told it so glibly and with just the right amount of poignancy that she almost believed the lies herself. When he had finished, the reporter asked, "Can I take some more pictures?"

"Only a few, and then I'm going to have to ask you to leave. The Parrishes are going to Santa Fe this afternoon, and we want to spend as much time as possible with them."

"Yeah, sure. Anything, Mr. Sloan." Now that he had the scoop of the week, Bob Scott was suddenly humble and obsequious.

For the next few minutes Lauri suffered through having pictures taken with Drake, and a few with Jennifer. She felt like a fool, acting out a charade and agonizing over how they would undo the damage the story would create.

Just as the reporter was packing up his gear, Betty Groves came running into the room from the kitchen. "What is going on, Lauri?" she asked with her characteristic breathlessness. "I saw all those cars in the driveway. We just got back from Albuquerque." Lauri had been glad that Betty was spending a few days with relatives. It had saved her from having to introduce Betty to her parents, which, under the circumstances, could have proved awkward.

Now, as Betty stood there with her bright, curious grin and her round, flashing eyes, Lauri felt that she was in a bad dream that went on and on relentlessly. What else could happen? As if in answer to her question, Sam and Sally whirled into the room like miniature tornadoes and pounced on Jennifer, who greeted her friends with equal zest.

"Who are all these people?" Betty asked over the children's squeals.

Drake threw up his hands in a gesture of hopeless abdication and laughed loudly. Andrew and Alice stood up and walked over to Betty to introduce themselves.

To add to the confusion Bob Scott was flashing pictures as quickly as his camera would allow.

"Her parents?" Lauri heard Betty exclaim. "Well, nice to—"

". . . their wedding . . ." She heard her mother's voice.

". . . married . . ." That from Andrew.

"God, what a mess." This from Drake, spoken under his breath.

Then she was being embraced by Betty's plump arms. "You're married! Oh, Lauri! Drake! Oh, I'm so happy for you! I said all along—ask Jim if I didn't—that you two belonged together. I just knew you were in love! And little Jennifer! What did she think about it? Oh, I think I'm going to cry!" And with that, Betty burst into tears and cried copiously until long after Drake had escorted Bob Scott to his car.

The grateful reporter promised the "happy couple" a front-page picture and the foldout story, complete with color pictures. Drake spoke in terse sentences as he nicely, but firmly, packed Mr. Scott into his car.

Betty graciously offered to take Jennifer home with her for a while so Lauri, Drake, and the Parrishes could have a respite from all the excitement. The Parrishes went to their room to begin packing their things. They would need to leave within an hour to make the first meeting of the pastors' conference scheduled for that night.

Lauri retreated upstairs and stripped off her clothes. She stepped into the shower and stood under the pounding pressure of the hot water, hoping it might relieve some of the pent-up tension.

When she finally turned off the taps and opened the clear glass door to reach for a towel, she pulled herself up sharply when she saw Drake standing in the doorway watching her.

She grabbed the towel and hugged it to her. "Don't bother. I've already seen everything there is to see," he said huskily and started toward her.

"All right. I won't," Lauri declared harshly as she began to dry herself. Something in the angry set of her shoulders and chin halted him. She did the job thoroughly, mechanically, ignoring him, and that disconcerted him more than if she had run for cover.

"I warned you once about walking around the house that way," he said.

"I was taking a shower. I didn't expect an audience."

When she finished drying herself, she took a pair of panties out of a drawer and stepped into them, easing them over her smooth, trim thighs. Drake leaned against the dressing table, never taking his eyes off her.

She reached in the drawer and took out a lacy bra. Before she could put it on, he yanked it out of her hand and flung it to the floor. Her only reaction was to shrug indifferently and pull on her sweater without the benefit of the undergarment. Still taking no notice of him, she put on a pair of slacks she had brought with her into the bathroom.

No sooner had she zipped them when Drake lunged

at her and embraced her fiercely. His lips bruised hers as they crashed onto them. His hands wandered restlessly over her back. She employed every ounce of discipline she possessed not to respond to him and held herself rigid. Finally he lifted his head and said, "You're upset."

She pushed away from him. "You might say that." Picking up a hairbrush, she began pulling it through her hair.

"Things got a little out of hand, didn't they?" he asked after long moments of silence.

"Yes, they did." She put the hairbrush down on the dressing table and faced him squarely. "Do you have any conception of the havoc you've wreaked on my life? My parents' life? Don't you care for anyone but yourself?" She drew a long, shuddering breath. "I'll apologize for my mother's blunder, though at least it was an honest mistake. None of this would have happened if you hadn't told that blatant lie in the first place." Her chin was tilted back in an angle of defiance.

"Have I placed the blame with anyone else?" he asked quietly. "Is this where I should say something like 'Your sins will find you out' or 'You reap what you sow'?"

"You always know your lines, don't you?" She stalked past him angrily on her way out of the bathroom, but his hand closed around her arm and drew her against him.

"Lauri, you little firebrand. Always on the defensive, always spoiling for a fight. For once why don't you just surrender?" His lips brushed across her temple. "Hasn't it occurred to you that I might like the idea of everyone thinking you were my wife? It would certainly protect me from the gossip-mongers. And we could—"

She shoved away from him with such force that he was stunned. "We could what?" she fairly screamed. "We could go on living in this make-believe world that you've constructed?" she laughed bitterly. "Your arrogance and conceit and insensitivity are a constant source of amazement to me, Drake. Do you think for one moment that I would pretend to be your wife?"

He turned his back on her and thrust his hands in his pockets in a gesture she knew well. He used it to withdraw into himself. It revealed one small chink in the wall, a particle of vulnerability.

"I had a wife," he muttered. "I told you—"

"Oh, yes," she scoffed. "You told me all about your wife. You loved her. And now you want no emotional entanglements."

She went up to his back and forcibly turned him around so he would have to face her. "Well, let me tell *you* something for a change. I don't want to be your wife, pretend or otherwise. I find your proposal unappealing, Mr. *Sloan*. And I can't for the life of me understand your persistent attempts to get me into your bed. Don't you think it will be crowded in there with you, me, and your wife's ghost?"

The skin on his cheekbones stretched so tautly and the lines around his mouth hardened so visibly that Lauri was afraid he might strike her. He gripped her shoulders painfully and jerked her against him. She could feel the fury that boiled inside him.

"Lauri, Drake, I'd like to speak with you both a moment if I may." Andrew's voice accompanied a timid knock on the bedroom door.

It took several seconds for the interruption to penetrate Drake's rage, but slowly she felt the hands on her arms relax until he dropped them to his sides.

"Daddy," she said waveringly, "what do you want?"

"I hate to bother you, but it's important. At least to Mother and me it is."

Lauri cast a wary eye over her shoulder at Drake as she went into the bedroom and said, "Come in."

Andrew hastened into the room and apologized again for barging in on them. "We have to leave soon, and I wondered if you'd indulge the whim of an old man."

Out of the corner of her eye, Lauri saw Drake come up to stand beside her. She crossed her arms over her chest as if for protection. "What is it, Daddy?" she asked in a deceptively calm voice.

"I always felt that you and Paul would have had a better chance if you'd been married by me in our church. I know it's old-fashioned," he said hurriedly when she started to protest. "Please, Lauri, Drake, let me perform a brief wedding ceremony for you before I leave."

Chapter Eleven

❦

Lauri stared at her father, taking in the import of his words. Drake was standing close beside her. She could almost feel his eyes on the top of her head as they looked down at her. Her father was waiting for her to say something. She laughed nervously and said, "Daddy, that's not necessary."

"I know that, Lauri, but please humor me. Your mother and I hated having you marry someone we had never met in a cold civil ceremony. When your marriage turned out to be so unhappy for you—and don't try to tell me it wasn't, I know it was—we felt responsible for not being more involved with you and your husband. This time, I want to be a part of your marriage, your family."

His eyes softened, and he reached out and took her clammy hand in both of his. "It was always my greatest wish that I marry both you and Ellen. I performed her wedding ceremony, remember?" Tears were clogging her throat as she nodded. "Please let me sanction yours to Drake."

Lauri tried to speak, but her chest was too congested; tears blurred her eyes. How she hated deceiving this kind, loving man who had given her life and wanted only her happiness. She opened her mouth to tell him the truth, but her lips felt rubbery and refused to be controlled.

She felt the strong support of Drake's arm as he placed it around her shoulders. "We'd be honored, sir. I speak for both of us."

"Good. Good," Andrew said, bringing his hands together in a hearty clasp that made a clapping sound. His gray eyes shone merrily. "I'll go tell Mother. She'll be so pleased. We'll be downstairs waiting for you." He left the room quickly and shut the door behind him.

It was debatable who took the initiative, but Lauri found herself wrapped in Drake's arms with her face buried in the curve of his shoulder. All the frustration, anger, and guilt came pouring out in a torrent of tears until his shirt front was damp from the onslaught.

He said nothing, but only lent his support and comfort. Stroking the auburn head and patting her back, he waited until her tears were spent and she rested against him, deflated and despairing.

Her words were muffled as she spoke, and he lowered his head over hers in an effort to hear her. "I'm a hypocrite of the worst sort. I rail at you for the lie you told, but I perpetuate that lie with everything I do." She sniffed loudly. "It's just that I couldn't stand to hurt him."

"Whether you believe this or not, and I doubt that you do, I don't want to see them disillusioned by me either. When I saw that you were trying to find the courage to tell him the truth, I couldn't let it happen. I had to intervene."

He pushed her from him gently and wiped away the tears that still lingered on her cheeks. "Let's go through this wedding ceremony with dignity. We'll know it doesn't mean anything. It's not legal. Later on we'll figure out something to tell them." He saw a flash of anger flare in her eyes and anticipated its source. "I won't desert you. I'll take the responsibility too. Now, go wash your face. They're waiting for us." He kissed her lightly on the forehead before she went to restore her face.

"I now pronounce you man and wife. What God has joined together, let no man put asunder." Andrew intoned the words that, had it been legal, would have linked her life to Drake's. "You may kiss your bride, son."

Drake placed his hands on her shoulders and turned her toward him. His eyes traveled over her face, trying to read it before he leaned down and kissed her sweetly on the lips. It was a brief kiss, but it was potent, and Lauri felt its impact throughout her body.

They were surrounded by Andrew and Alice, and Betty and the three children, who Alice had insisted be present. She had called Betty and told her to come over for the ceremony. Betty had cried through the short nuptials, but the children had stood quietly, listening in awe and watching Andrew's hands as he reverently signed the words for Jennifer's benefit. Likewise, Lauri and Drake had used sign for their vows.

At any other time, Lauri would have thought it was the most beautiful marriage ceremony ever. Even if the setting and clothes weren't traditional, she discovered that as she said the vows to Drake, she meant them. It was a moving realization. She pledged him her love and faithfulness of body as well as of spirit, and it wasn't because the witnesses expected her to say the correct words. It was because she wanted to say them to Drake and have him know that she meant them.

Her lips verbalized what her heart already knew. This deep, unbearable, sweet longing she felt for Drake was love. Love. Yes, she loved him. She could see his faults, and recognize his temperament, but they didn't change her feelings. He provoked her anger as no one else could, but still she loved him.

It would be in vain, Lauri cautioned herself. For he had loved once—he had loved deeply and eternally—and there was no room in his heart for any other woman except the dead Susan. He had been honest with Lauri; she could be no less. She confessed her love, if not to him, then to herself.

Drake kissed Betty soundly on the mouth and she

swooned theatrically. Then he was laughing and hugging Alice and shaking hands with Andrew who thumped him on the back. He knelt down and lifted Jennifer in his arms and snuggled her against him, tickling her cheek with his mustache, an action that always made her giggle.

One would almost believe that this was a happy occasion for everyone until they saw the bride's face. It was pale, and periodically her whole body would shudder as if she were trying forcibly to keep a tight rein on her emotions.

A short time later the Parrishes took their leave. Their luggage had been placed in the trunk of the rental car, and they stood on the front porch saying their final goodbyes.

Alice had tears in her eyes as she kissed Jennifer, who returned the kiss without reservation. Lauri embraced her parents in turn, clinging to them as if they were a lifeline. When they were in the car and it was moving down the steep lane leading from the house, they waved and called good-byes and promises to telephone and write. And all the while Drake stood beside Lauri, playing the loving husband. In one arm he held Jennifer. The other was secure around Lauri's waist.

"Boy, what a day, Jennifer," Drake said with a sigh as he collapsed on the sofa and lifted his daughter onto his lap. "Lauri, don't cook anything for dinner. Let's snack tonight. I know you must be tired too."

"All right, Drake. I'll just put a few things out." She

went into the kitchen hastily. Why was she suddenly nervous about being in the same room with him?

After they had eaten the light meal, Jennifer was bathed and put to bed. She had been wearied by the events of the day and began to show her fatigue during mealtime, when she became petulant.

Lauri was relieved when the querulous child was tucked in for the night. She returned to the kitchen to load the dishwasher, but saw that Drake had preceded her. The job was almost finished.

"You shouldn't have bothered, Drake. I would have cleaned this up."

He smiled over his shoulder. "You had Jennifer to cope with. I took the easy way out."

"She was exhausted. It's unlike her to behave so badly, especially when you're around. I hope she's not getting sick."

He laughed as he came up to her and put his arms around her. "You sound just like a mother," he whispered roughly into her hair.

"Do I?" she asked coolly. She pushed away from him and went to the kitchen sink, acting busy as she filled a glass with water and brought it to her lips.

He was undaunted by her lack of response and came up behind her, bracing himself against the countertop by placing his hands on either side of her. With his nose he pushed the hair on her neck out of his way and began to tease her skin with love bites.

"Drake—"

"This is so incredibly soft," he murmured. A thrill shot through her when she felt the tip of his tongue caressing the back of her earlobe.

"Please, Drake—" She struggled to turn around, and when he did relent, it was only to allow her to face him. Now her hips were pressed against the counter, and he held her imprisoned with his solid body.

He took her hands and placed them on his chest, flattening her palms until she could feel the beat of his heart, the warmth that radiated from his skin, and the crinkling texture of his chest hair under the soft fabric.

"Lauri, do you realize that in some cultures the marriage isn't even considered legal until the couple is married in church and the union blessed by God? In that case we are married. Civil ceremonies often count for nothing."

His hands were sifting through her hair. He settled his fingers on her scalp and massaged her temples with his thumbs in a mesmerizing rhythm.

Starting at her forehead, he kissed it with tenderness before moving over her closed eyelids to her cheeks. Each kiss was slow and deliberate, as if he were embedding his lips in her skin.

He sipped at her lips, tempting them, tantalizing them, before he took them completely under his. His tongue didn't countenance the barrier of lips and teeth as he gratified its driving desire to plunder her mouth. He

Sandra Brown

moved against her. It was physically apparent that his kiss only symbolized an all-consuming desire to possess her totally.

Her legs had been rendered useless by his entrapment; the muscles in them had turned to water. But her arms were imbued with strength as she slid them up his chest and closed them around his neck. She moved closer yet, feeling his hard length in delicious contrast to the soft contours of her own body. She was again made aware of that perfect fit, the complement of his maleness to her femaleness.

"Lauri," he rasped, "you suspend me somewhere between Heaven and Hell. But I swear that this Hell is sweeter than anything I've ever known." He ravaged her neck, but she was a willing victim, submitting to his lips and teeth and tongue, which seemed to know her with more intimacy than she knew herself. They didn't seek vulnerable spots, but knew them instinctively and went to them directly and with unflagging purpose.

She could be his wife in every sense of the word. She wanted to be, and in her mind she already was. Morally her conscience was clear. Before God and a licensed minister, she had pledged her life and love to this man. Nothing could shake her conviction that the vows she had made to him were valid and binding.

But he had made no such vows.

He had recited the poetic words, repeated the familiar lines, but he hadn't spoken them from his heart. In order to protect her and out of respect for her parents, he had played his role and played it convincingly. Lauri, however, knew his motivation, and it wasn't love. His love was lost to him forever, buried in a grave, and there was nothing she could do about it.

He needed her now. She could sense desperation in the way he held her. The intensity with which he kissed her was an indication of his passion. If she accepted his lovemaking now, how long would it take for that passion to wane? How long before he would withdraw into a world of his own as Paul had? When she needed the salve of his love to soothe her wounds, would he be there? She couldn't take the chance. She would rather live without his love entirely than to live with a facsimile of it.

It was several moments before Drake realized that her frantic movements weren't born of passion. She was fighting him. It so surprised him that he released her immediately. She pushed past him and ran from the room. When she was halfway up the stairs, he called her name.

His voice was soft, but more compelling because of it. "Lauri."

She halted in midstride on the step. She didn't turn around. If she looked at him, she would be lost. Even now, if only he'd say that he loved her, she would fly into his arms and find surcease from this torment that gripped her. *Say you love me*! she cried silently.

"Lauri—" He bit off any other words and seemed to hesitate. A simple "Good night" was the dejected valediction.

Something had awakened Lauri. She was lifted out of a deep sleep with the intuitive knowledge that something was wrong. Listening for a moment, she could hear nothing that would have awakened her, but nonetheless she flung off the covers and got out of bed. Her robe was lying across a chair, and she pulled it on before she stepped into the darkened hallway.

Her first thought was of Jennifer. She went to the door of the little girl's room. The bed was empty. Lauri suppressed the panic that swept over her and crossed the room toward the adjoining bath. Jennifer wasn't in there either.

Stumbling over the hem of her robe in her haste, she descended the stairs and checked the rooms on the first floor. No Jennifer. Thinking—hoping—the child may have gotten up for a drink of water or a cookie, she went into the kitchen and switched on the light. Jennifer wasn't in the room, but the back door was standing open, letting in the cold night air. Lauri's heart stopped.

Kidnapped!

That was her first thought. Drake was a celebrity. He and his daughter would be the perfect targets for a perverted mind who was seeking instant wealth or notoriety.

Her first impulse was to dash headlong out the door

and find the child herself, but she stopped halfway across the room. What if they were still out there? They could overpower her. It was dark and cold. She had no weapon.

She ran into Drake's room and without hesitation placed her hand on his bare shoulder and shook him hard.

"Drake, wake up." Was that her voice that was quivering in fear? It sounded almost like a sob. "Drake, please wake up."

He bolted upright and looked at her with the wild, vacant, startled eyes of a man stunned out of sleep. "Lauri? Wh—what is it?"

"Jennifer. She's gone. I woke up—heard something, I think—back door. I thought, maybe kidnappers—"

She was stuttering and making no sense whatsoever, but he recognized terror when he saw it, and he caught enough of her words to interpolate the rest.

He kicked away the covers and flew out of the bed with one fluid, animallike motion.

He grabbed his velour wrapper from a hook on the back of the door and shrugged into it as he hurried after Lauri, who was already returning to the kitchen.

He went directly to the door and peered out into the inky darkness. "Should we call the police?" Lauri asked tremulously as she wrung her hands. "Drake, what—" She couldn't continue. She was sobbing.

"Calm down, Lauri. Hysterics won't help. Yes, call the police. I'll go out to the shed and get a flashlight—"

"But they may still be out there. Oh, Drake, no—"

"Who's 'they'? We don't even know what happened. But I swear to God, if anything's happened to Jennifer, I'll kill—"

"Are you looking for the Midnight Prowler?"

The two frantic people standing in the middle of the room turned with one motion and stared open-mouthed at Betty, who held Jennifer in her arms.

"Oh, God," Lauri said, clamping a hand over her mouth in relief and then rushing to retrieve the child from Betty's arms. She hugged Jennifer to her and rocked her back and forth, still not believing that she was safely at home.

"What happened?" Drake asked, and Lauri noted that his voice was none too steady. He had a protective hand on Jennifer's back.

"I was sound asleep," Betty explained, "when I heard someone at the back door. Of course, I just *knew* it was a burglar or a rapist and nearly panicked. I'll never get used to Jim being gone all the time and having to stay by myself." Her round brown eyes kept straying to the disturbing sight of Drake's bare chest, exposed by the deep V of the velour robe.

"Well, anyway," Betty continued, "I decided that it wasn't a very smart rapist because he sure was making a lot of racket trying to open the door. I guess I was more curious than scared. I went into the kitchen and peeked out the window. Jennifer was standing on the step trying to open the door. When I let her in, she made a beeline for Sally's room. She had left Bunny there this afternoon. When she got what she came for, she started back home. I thought I'd better come with her and make sure she got here safely. Can you imagine that little stinker going out alone in the middle of the night without so much as a by-your-leave?"

"She was so tired when she went to bed, she probably didn't miss Bunny. When she woke up in the middle of the night and realized he wasn't with her, she went to get him." Lauri filled in the rest of the story. She was smiling at the child, who was snuggling Bunny and yawning sleepily. Lauri pushed the tangled curls away from the dimpled cheeks as she kissed them.

Drake reached for his daughter and stood her in front of him as he knelt down. "Jennifer, that was very naughty!" he signed in a way that emphasized his spoken message. "Never run away from me or Lauri. It makes us—" He groped for *scared* and looked to Lauri for help. She gave him the sign and he continued, "It makes us scared and sad. We didn't know where you were. If you ever run away again, I'll have to spank you."

Jennifer's bottom lip began to tremble, and she knew her daddy was serious about what he said. Then his arms went around her and he held on to her tightly, squeezing his eyes shut in agony over thoughts of what could have happened. Jennifer's arms went around his neck, though she still kept a firm grip on Bunny. Drake lifted her and they walked out of the kitchen.

"My goodness, I—"

"Thank you, Betty. I can't tell you how relieved I

was to see you with her. I had just roused Drake, and we were naturally imagining the worst.'' She was grateful to her neighbor but wasn't up to one of Betty's exuberant monologues.

"I've got to get back to my kids. Good night. You get back upstairs to your little family.'' She touched Lauri's arm in a comforting gesture and scurried out the back door. Lauri made certain it was locked. She hadn't recovered from her fright.

In Jennifer's room Drake was sitting on the edge of her bed, stroking his daughter's forehead, though she had already drifted peacefully to sleep. He took Lauri's hand as she leaned down and kissed the child.

They left the room together. When they reached the hallway, Drake observed, "You're shivering."

"I don't know if it's from the cold or fear."

"Would you like a glass of wine or something?"

"No, I'll be fine,'' she said as they reached the door to the master bedroom. She looked up at him and smiled, but her smile faded when she saw the naked hunger on his face that was too arresting to turn away from.

They faced each other and stared for long moments. He didn't touch her, but he didn't have to. She was vividly aware of his body, which seemed to gravitate toward hers, though he hadn't moved. Like magnets with opposite poles, they were drawn inexorably together. Their instinctive, undeniable need for each other was a force suddenly unmitigated by reason. When they did move together, they held each other tightly, clinging to each other in a desperate fear of separation.

She didn't resist when he scooped her in his arms and carried her into the bedroom, laying her gently against the pillows. In one swift motion he was free of his robe and briefs. Splendidly naked, he lay down beside her with the sensuous ease of a pagan god practicing a love rite.

"Lauri, don't talk. Don't think. For God's sake, don't *think*. Only feel. Feel."

His hands reacquainted themselves with the curves of her body. He took his time, sliding the fabric of her robe against her skin. But he wanted to see and know it all, and he separated the folds of her robe, raising her shoulders as he slipped it from her body.

He pulled her to him and held her with a fierce possession that was tempered by gentleness. His mouth fastened on hers while his hands sculpted her flesh, molding it, and breathing life into it.

Her shoulders, breasts, and stomach knew his touch and reveled in it. He knelt over her and kissed her breasts with hot, swollen lips. The part of her that deemed her woman arched against his hand when he placed his palm over her. He found her waiting for him, moist and warm with longing.

His touch was the height of tenderness, and so sublimely intimate that Lauri sobbed and clasped his shoulders in celebration of a feeling she had never before shared.

"Lauri. You are a beautiful . . . woman . . . made for me." His words were disjointed, but had he not spoken at all, Lauri would have known what he was thinking. His caressing lips and the reverence of his touch told her everything she needed to know.

Paul's words came back to haunt her. She had never pleased him. Now she realized she hadn't cared enough to want to. But she wanted to make Drake's body sing as hers was.

Her hands roamed over the taut flesh, kneading the muscles her hands encountered. She cast off her cloak of modesty and inhibition and touched him, thrilling to his virility.

"Lauri . . . yes, darling. Learn me," he gasped as he burrowed his head in her neck and clasped her tightly.

His reaction gave her confidence, and Paul's insulting words disintegrated into oblivion when she heard Drake's muffled cries of pleasure. He repeated her name in a whispered chant, his breath sighing in her ear.

He cupped her face in the palms of his hands and captured her mouth with his own in a deep kiss. Hesitating, he poised on the brink of absolute possession. He raised his head and looked down at her. She brought one of her hands to his face and traced the handsome features she had come to love. Her fingers smoothed over the silken mustache and circled his lips. Their eyes were unwavering.

"Lauri?" he breathed.

She felt his initial touch. Closing her eyes, she drew

his head down beside hers on the pillow. She sighed his name in wonderment when she knew all of him.

And the glory of it was that it didn't stop there, as it always had before. Whispering acclamations, Drake savored her. The tumult in her body grew, encompassing her heart and expanding into her soul. He uttered her name in an exultant cry when his passion was made manifest. She heard it a heartbeat before a volcano erupted within her.

And the explosions went on . . . and on . . . and on.

"That's never happened to me before," she whispered timidly into the darkness.

Her head rested on Drake's chest as he held her against him, their legs entwined under the covers. Absently he stroked her back.

"Never?" he asked softly, proudly. "Not with—"

"Paul? No," she said with a sad smile and shook her head slightly. The hairs on his chest tickled her nose. "I didn't think I could," she confessed.

A laugh rumbled in his chest and was amplified in her ear. "Well, now we know better, don't we?" He swatted her on the fanny, then his hand remained and turned the playful gesture into a caress.

She should be feeling remorse over what had happened, but she couldn't conjure up that sentiment. Indeed, she wasn't sorry at all. For what she had done had been out of love. And she knew that she would continue making love to Drake. It was inevitable now, and she no longer had the ambition or will to fight it. She nestled closer to him.

"Are you cold?" he asked solicitously.

"A little," she said.

"All the covers got kicked to the foot of the bed," he said with feigned puzzlement.

"I wonder how," she giggled.

They soon had the covers settled over them. Drake nuzzled her ear as he drew her close. "I promise not to disturb the covers this time."

"This time?" she asked incredulously. "You mean again? Now?"

"Don't you want to?" he asked. Even in the darkness she could see the eyebrow arched cockily over his eye.

"Well, I—"

But his head had already lowered and his mouth was persuasive. She heard herself agree in a small but urgent voice, "Yes, yes."

Chapter Twelve

❦

The next several days were idyllic. Drake proved to be an ardent lover and rarely let Lauri out of his sight. Sharing a room wasn't enough. He had to be touching her, if not with his hands, with his eyes. Their nights were filled with a passion that they both marveled at. During the day, when Jennifer was with them, they communicated their happiness to the child, and she basked in the glow of it.

They went into the village often, milling through the shops that lined the hilly, picturesque streets. One afternoon they visited John Meadows in his woodcrafts shop. He welcomed them warmly and gave no indication that he remembered the rudeness Drake had exhibited when they had last met.

Lauri was gratified when Drake took a genuine interest in John's work and asked polite questions concerning the objects on display. The two men, so vastly diverse, chatted affably. However, Drake kept a possessive arm around Lauri's shoulders. It was a declaration of ownership that didn't go unnoticed.

They enjoyed their frequent outings, but their favorite times were the quiet evenings spent at home sitting near the fireplace and sharing their thoughts over a bottle of wine.

Lauri usually sat in the corner of the sofa while Drake stretched out on his back and lay his head in her lap as he had done the night her parents made their surprise visit. He outlined his ambitions, gesturing with expressive hands, his eyes fired by an inner resource.

But no matter how thought-provoking their topic, soon their conversation would wane. The hands that had punctuated his conversation would begin stroking and caressing her until the fire in the fireplace was nothing compared to the conflagration that burned between them.

When her parents called before their return trip to Nebraska, Lauri didn't have to pretend happiness. She urged them to stop in Whispers, but commitments compelled them to go home immediately after the pastors' conference. She hung up, assuring them that she was blissfully content. For, at that moment in time, she was.

They took long walks through the woods after Lauri and Jennifer had completed lessons and before Betty and the children came over for their sign class. Often Lauri would pack a picnic lunch for them, and they would sit on old blankets and eat leisurely beside a brook and under the aspens that were bare now with the approach of winter.

One bright afternoon on such an outing, when they had finished eating, Jennifer succumbed to the somnolent day and fell asleep, curled up on the blanket. Drake leaned his back against a tree and pulled Lauri between his raised knees, pressing her back into his wide chest.

"I may do what Jennifer's doing if I get any more comfortable," she murmured sleepily as she rested her head on his chest.

"Go ahead," he said into her hair and spread an extra blanket over them.

His steady breathing provided a lulling cadence she couldn't resist, and she was soon drowsing. In that region between sleep and wakefulness, disturbing thoughts invaded the tranquillity that encompassed her. For days she had pushed thoughts of Susan away. Drake's affection was undeniable, but even at the height of their passion, he had never once said that he loved her.

Had he and Susan ever sat like this? Had his lovemaking to her been more fervent? Would he ever be able to love Lauri with that same intensity? She must have stirred restlessly with these disturbing questions. Drake's arms went around her more firmly and he whispered, "Bad dreams?"

She shook her head no, but her musings had shattered the euphoria of the day and allowed a worm of doubt to creep into her consciousness.

Just when she was about to straighten up and pull away from him, she felt his hands exploring her. He settled his hands around her waist and slipped them between her sweater and the waistband of her jeans. That one suggestion was enough to begin those now familiar pangs of desire that made her languorous and malleable.

Her sweater was lifted slightly as he slid his hands underneath it. She felt his touch on her breasts; fondling, kneading. His caress was as gentle and inquiring as it had been the first time. He knew her body so well, yet made her feel like each time he touched her was a discovery.

"Drake?"

"Don't bother a man when he's busy," he growled against her ear.

Suddenly she was shy. If she couldn't tell him that she loved him, she wanted to say something that would let him know a measure of what she felt for him. "I just wanted you to know that every time you—we—are together—I—it's very special to me."

His hands ceased their movement and palmed her breasts gently. He was alarmingly still. "Lauri," he said huskily. "Look at me."

She leaned her head against his shoulder and tilted it back in order to see him. "It's very special to me too," he said. His mouth took hers in a kiss that made her veins throb with a heated flow of blood.

His hands slid down her ribs to her waist, then returned over her stomach to cup her breasts. He lifted them, teasing the aching nipples with his stroking thumbs, rolling them between his fingers while he nibbled her earlobe. It reminded her of the times he had captured those pink points in his teeth. She gave a soft cry and writhed against the questing hand that had slipped to her thigh.

When he fumbled with the snap on her jeans, she realized what was about to happen and was dismayed at her own abandon. She was struck with shyness and self-consciousness.

"Drake, no," she gasped and squirmed away from him. "Not out here," she said primly, straightening her clothing under the blanket.

"Why?" he asked, his eyes glinting mischievously. "It's fun in the woods, you know. Think of the Vikings, think of the Romans, think of Robin Hood and Lady Marian—"

"Well, I'm not any of them. Besides, your daughter is lying right there." She indicated the sleeping Jennifer with an inclination of her head. She was still holding his hands away from her and dared not let them go.

"She's asleep," he argued. "Come on, Lauri. Please." He was whining now and leaned over to brush her mouth with his mustache. It was a dangerous weapon, and he knew how to use it.

"No. What if someone came by?"

"They'd be embarrassed and look the other way."

"I'd be mortified!" she cried. Then she softened her tone and left it full of promise. "Can't you wait until tonight?" she asked provocatively.

"Well," he grumbled. "I guess I'll have to. You kiss me once and I'll kiss you and then we'll go home." She didn't see the gleam in his eyes, and it seemed like a reasonable request.

She turned to face him and kissed him on the mouth. It was a passionless kiss, but conveyed all the love she felt for him. When at last they drew apart, he said, "Now my turn."

"What are you doing?" She was shocked when he lifted the front of her sweater.

"I'm getting my kiss. I didn't say *what* I was going to kiss."

He raised the soft knit fabric and ducked his head under it. Leaving the peaks wet and aroused, he kissed first one breast then the other. When he looked at her again, he saw the auburn eyes swimming with tears of love. "One more, please," he said and closed his mouth over hers.

Lauri was unerringly certain of one thing. He hadn't been thinking of Susan.

"I've got some errands to run in town," Drake said, peering around the corner of the classroom the next morning. "Why don't I go do those and then pick up some homemade tamales for lunch. I met a lady the other day who makes them in her own kitchen. I sampled them, and they're fantastic."

Lauri laughed as he smacked his lips. "Well, if you like fat ladies, I guess I can eat tamales for lunch."

"I like you," he said gruffly, and raked her body with lascivious eyes. "I'll see you later," he promised wickedly. "Good-bye, Jennifer," he said to his daughter, who was busy stacking building blocks that had been used for a counting lesson. She responded and he left.

It was about a half hour before Drake was expected back when Lauri took Jennifer into the kitchen.

"You're going to like this, Jennifer," she said and sat the little girl down at the kitchen table.

"We're going to play a game to see if you can tell the difference between white milk and chocolate." As usual, Lauri was signing every word. Jennifer watched with interest. Food lessons were her favorite.

"Okay," Lauri continued, "I'll fill two glasses. See? One has white milk and the other chocolate. Let me see you say them." When Jennifer had satisfactorily signed *white milk* and *chocolate milk* and pronounced them as well as she could, Lauri said, "Now I'm going to give you a straw. I'll put each glass in front of you, and you tell me which kind of milk it is. Do you understand?"

Jennifer nodded, and the blond curls bounced around her head.

"Cover your eyes so you can't see," Lauri directed. When she was certain that Jennifer wasn't cheating,

Lauri placed the straw into the glass of white milk. Jennifer took a sip and then gave the correct sign. They repeated the exercise until Lauri was sure the child had a command of the words and could associate the taste with the name assigned it.

They had just completed the exercise when Drake came through the back door carrying a sack of the delicious-smelling tamales.

"What are you two doing?" he asked, setting the sack on the countertop and taking off his jacket.

Let's see if Drake can do it. Lauri addressed Jennifer, and the child clapped her hands happily. Lauri explained the rules of the game, and to Jennifer's delight Drake pretended to be unsure of his ability to do it correctly.

He made a big production of closing his eyes, but finally took a sip out of a straw and said in sign, *That's white milk.* However when Lauri reached for the glass of chocolate, she saw that Jennifer had almost drained it.

"Jennifer!" she admonished, but they were all laughing. Jennifer was pointing to her upper lip, which sported a dark brown chocolate mustache. She was comparing it to Drake's.

You too, Lauri, she signed. You too.

With much ado, Lauri protested, but Jennifer and Drake insisted. She picked up the glass of chocolate milk and took a big drink, making sure that some of it got on her upper lip. Jennifer let out a peal of laughter and jumped up and down. When they finally settled her down, Lauri instructed her, "Go upstairs and wash your face and hands while I fix our lunch." Jennifer skipped off happily.

"Aren't you going to wash your face?" Drake asked with a mocking smile. "The mustache clashes with your hair."

"Oh. I forgot all about it," she answered and turned toward the sink.

"Allow me," he said, taking her by the shoulders.

His velvet-rough tongue rid her of the milk mustache quickly, but as with all their kisses, the embrace was extended. Her arms went around him and they kissed for long minutes until both of them pulled away breathlessly.

"If we keep this up, you'll never get your lunch," she mumbled as her lips teased his chin.

"I may want to change the menu," he said thickly. He kissed her neck.

"The tamales will get cold." She sighed deeply when he found a sensitive spot.

"That's why they invented microwave ovens. Didn't you know that?" he muttered into her ear.

She drew a resigned breath and gently extricated herself from his arms. "Let's behave. Jennifer will be in here in a minute demanding her lunch."

"Where is that little scamp?" Drake asked. "I hope she hasn't run off again." His eyes warmed as they looked at Lauri. He was remembering, as she was, that the night Jennifer ran away, they were together for the first time.

"I'll go check on her," Lauri said quickly. "If you don't mind setting the table." He shook his head, and Lauri darted out of the room before she submitted to another embrace.

She climbed the stairs and was making her way to Jennifer's room when she saw movement in her own. Oh, please not another disaster, Lauri thought as she pushed the door open wider.

Then her heart stopped.

The first thing that caught her eye was the pair of pink satin ballet shoes. They would have fit dainty, slender feet with high arches. The shoes had no doubt been used a great deal for rehearsal, for the round, flat toes were well-worn, and the satin ribbons were wrinkled from frequent lacings.

The shoes were lying among pictures, clothes, several theater programs, and a large, leather-bound scrapbook. Lauri's stunned eyes took in the open closet door from which the storage boxes had been taken.

Jennifer sat on the floor staring at one of the pictures in solemn concentration. Slowly, on legs of lead, Lauri walked over to her and attracted her attention.

Lauri, see? Pretty lady, she signed and indicated the picture in her hand.

With a trembling hand Lauri reached for the picture and stared down at the woman immortalized in the photograph. She was beautiful. She was wearing practice clothes. The woolly leg warmers that are almost a part of a dancer's anatomy hugged the shapely calves and accented the perfection of her thighs.

She was leaning against the barre as if at rest from pliés and tendus. She stared directly into the camera, unaffected and unposed, challenging the photographer's lens to detect a flaw. Her hair was dark, parted down the middle, and smoothed into a chignon at the base of her swanlike neck. The dark eyes were the largest and most arresting feature of her heart-shaped face.

"Yes, she's pretty," Lauri said in a barely audible voice. Quite unconsciously she had dropped to the floor beside Jennifer. Her shoulders slumped dejectedly at her first sight of the woman who still possessed Drake's heart.

"Hey, you two, I'm starving. What's going on up there?" Drake's happy bantering jolted Lauri out of her reverie, but before she could recover, he was standing in the doorway. His eyes and face were lighted up with a smile, but when he saw the disarray—the boxes with their contents strewn about without respect for their former owner, the child and the woman who had defiled the memory of his wife—his features hardened into a grim mask.

Lauri turned away from the sight of it; she couldn't witness that terrible pain. She retrieved the ballet shoes from Jennifer, who was trying them on her own feet.

Jennifer, go wash your face and hands, Lauri said with as much poise as she could. Jennifer started to protest and reached for the shoes again, but Lauri said, "Go!" The force of the command brooked no argument, and Jennifer walked past her father, who was standing over a photograph and staring at it, oblivious to everything around him.

When the child had left the room, Lauri said, "I'm sorry, Drake. She was meddling, I guess. I'll pick—"

"No, you won't," he snapped. "Leave everything where it is. I'll clear it up and put it away."

Lauri dropped the pink satin shoes as if they had burned her hand. "Very well," she said, and fled the room.

Drake was still standing in the middle of the floor staring down at the scattered photographs.

Lauri fixed Jennifer a peanut butter and jelly sandwich. The child chattered to Bunny, who sat on the table beside her plate as she ate it. Lauri gave her anything she grunted at and pointed to. This habit was taboo at any other time, but at the moment Lauri was too drained of energy to care.

When Jennifer had finished her lunch, Sam and Sally arrived at the back door to invite her to their house to play. Lauri wrapped her in a sweater—the one Drake had bought her on their trip to Albuquerque—and asked Sam to see that she got back in half an hour.

"Sure. We have to take our nap then anyway," he said as he led Jennifer down the steps to the yard.

Lauri watched them scamper across the yard, but she

wasn't really seeing them. Imprinted on the back of her eyelids were the pictures of the ballerina who gazed into the camera with such self-assurance.

What had caused her to die? Drake had never said. He avoided the subject of his wife completely. Lauri knew nothing about her except that she had been a dancer, a classical ballerina who had auditioned for the chorus of *Grease* and, at that audition, met the man she was to marry.

Had she been killed in an accident? An airplane crash? Had she contracted a dreadful disease that had cost her her life? A stroke? Surely not in one so young. What had happened to her?

Lauri cleared away the dishes Jennifer had used. She took the sack of tamales outside to the large trash barrel. The house was silent. She roamed the rooms, looking for something to do to fill the void in her soul, but there was nothing. She counted the minutes until Jennifer came back, and when she did, Lauri suggested that they look at a book. Jennifer went into the classroom and chose one on different types of transportation.

They sat on the sofa and discussed the cars, buses, airplanes, and boats in the large picture-book. Drake had been upstairs for two hours before Lauri heard his tread on the stairs.

She braced herself for anything. What would he be like now? How would he react to what had happened? When she faced him, she knew.

He was wearing slacks, a sport coat, and a tie: rare

attire for him since his coming to New Mexico. In his left hand he carried a valise. A trench coat was slung over his right shoulder.

Lauri stood up at his approach and clasped her hands together at her waist. It had come.

"Lauri, I'm going back to New York," he said succinctly.

"Yes."

He diverted his eyes away from her. "I've been here too long," he said. Was he convincing her or himself? "There are things I need to do. I can't stay here indefinitely."

"No." If he wanted her approval, he was in for a disappointment. She wasn't about to make it easy for him. She had begged Paul to let her help him. Her offers had been spurned: one rejection was enough. She wouldn't let Drake rub salt in the wounds.

"You'll explain my leaving to Jennifer?" he asked, not really expecting Lauri to reply. When she did, her answer surprised him.

"No. You'll explain it to her." He recognized the proud, haughty tilt of her chin and knew it was useless to argue.

He set his valise on the floor and knelt down in front of his daughter, who was still engrossed in the book. "Jennifer," Drake said. That's all Lauri heard. She went quickly to the front door and pressed her forehead against the hard cold wood. *I can't stand this*, she cried silently. *I'll die when he leaves*, she groaned. But when she heard his approaching footsteps, she righted herself and faced him with a bravado she was far from feeling.

"She's upset. Please reassure and comfort her for me," he said. And who'll comfort me? Lauri wanted to ask him. She noticed that he wasn't looking too stable himself. If she didn't know better, she would think that the strange shine in his eyes was caused by tears. Was he that upset over leaving his daughter? Or was this just a poignant farewell scene he was aptly playing?

"I have to take the car, but I'll arrange for someone to drive it back to you tomorrow."

She nodded.

"Well, good-bye, then. I'll be in touch." He acted as if there were more he wanted to say. Or— No, he couldn't have wanted to kiss her, though she thought his head had dipped slightly lower in a tentative attempt.

"Good-bye, Drake," she said flatly, and opened the front door for him.

The lines around his mouth tightened into a frown, and the thick brows lowered ominously. He sighed in exasperation before he shoved past her. She closed the door behind him.

Appropriately enough, gray clouds scuttled over the mountaintops and hung over the village of Whispers. They sifted down the first snow of the season. Somehow the pristine blanket of white did nothing to relieve the gloom that permeated the house.

Jennifer was disinclined to participate in any activity,

and Lauri allowed her to watch television for the rest of the day.

When bedtime finally came, the little girl hugged Bunny to her and repeated over and over in her sweet but almost incoherent voice, "Daud-y." Tears flowed down her rosy cheeks. It was too much for Lauri's shattered emotions. She lay down beside Jennifer and clasped her tight.

They cried themselves to sleep.

Chapter Thirteen

❦

Time dulled the heartache that Lauri and Jennifer suffered over Drake's leaving, though it was still prevalent if they were reminded of him. With the resilience of a child, Jennifer awoke the next morning chattering, excited over the snow, and eager to start a new day. As much for her own peace of mind as for Jennifer's, Lauri launched them into several projects that would be exhausting and fill the long hours of the day. They seemed to have multiplied since Drake left.

"I can't believe that he left you so soon after your wedding," Betty observed from her position on the kitchen stool. Lauri was supervising the making of popcorn balls. The children were sticky from their fingertips

225

to their elbows and stuffing the gooey mess in their mouths before the hot syrup had time to cool.

Lauri parried the remark, shrugging her shoulders negligently and saying, "He has a job, Betty. He had to get back."

"I know, but you've got to admit, it's strange behavior for a man on his honeymoon."

But Drake's not really on his honeymoon, Lauri thought to herself as Betty reread *The Scoop Sheet* for the third time.

She had purchased the magazine that morning while grocery shopping and rushed it over to Lauri. The laughing couple captured on the front page in glorious color was to Lauri an obscene mockery. She hadn't wanted to know what the article said, but Betty had read it aloud to her, missing the tears that slid from Lauri's eyes and rolled down her face. What had Drake thought of the false story? Had he even seen it?

For some reason she couldn't name, Lauri didn't want to disclose that she and Drake weren't actually married. Betty would never understand the complexities of the situation and barrage her with questions too painful to answer. Like her parents, Betty would have to stay ignorant of the true state of affairs a while longer.

Sooner or later they would all know the truth. Lauri would feel like an absolute fool, but no more than she already did. In the days following their mock wedding she had almost convinced herself that Drake was as much in love with her as she with him. He couldn't have been more loving, more devoted to making her happy.

She should have remembered his occupation. He was paid a tremendous amount of money to convey emotions every day. His role had demanded that he act like a loving newlywed, and he had played the part well. He had also been paid. Each night he had been paid in full on the king-size bed upstairs. That's all he had wanted from her in the first place.

Now she blushed furiously with anger and shame. He had told her at the beginning of their relationship what she could expect. Yet, she had deluded herself into thinking that she could change his need for her, could transform it into something deeper than physical longing.

It wasn't her aim to make him forget Susan. He would never forget, nor should he. Lauri only wanted him to be able to love again—to love her. She had thought she was about to succeed. Then she had seen his face as he looked down at the photographs of his first wife. The clothes strewn about the bedroom floor must have been vivid reminders of the woman who had worn them and danced in the satin shoes. His agony had been plain to see. Did he feel that he had betrayed Susan by sleeping with Lauri? Is that why he left?

As much as she tried to thrust these plaguing thoughts to the dark recesses of her brain, they adamantly remained in the forefront, torturing her. If it weren't for Jennifer's sweet disposition, she would have gone mad. At least Jennifer accepted her love and returned it in full. Lauri didn't even want to think of what it would do to her and the child when she left.

Left? Yes, she would have to leave if Drake were to come back. She couldn't resume their relationship as it was. Never could she be his mistress, sleeping with him whenever the mood struck him. She had been little more than that to Paul, and as she knew well, that was a dead-end street.

It looked as if she would have to bide her time to see what Drake expected of her. Jennifer received one or two brief notes each week, but he enclosed nothing for her. Not one word. He never called. Had he forgotten her entirely?

Two weeks extended into three and then into four. The weather prohibited most of their usual jaunts, so Lauri devised indoor projects. They painted with water-colors; they strung beads; they baked until the freezer was well stocked with cookies and cakes.

One day, as they were icing a chocolate cake, Lauri asked Jennifer if she would like to share it with John Meadows. Jennifer enthusiastically agreed.

The day was clear but extremely cold. They bundled up in their heavy coats and walked down to the village. John was working in his deserted shop. He wasn't busy these days. Whispers wasn't a skiing community, and the tourists were occupied in other villages that catered to the sport.

He was delighted to see them. Not expecting any

customers, John closed the shop and invited them to his living quarters in the back of the building.

"Here, Jennifer," Lauri said, giving the little girl a large piece of cake. "It's hard to invent teaching projects in the wintertime," she said, explaining their generosity. "Jennifer enjoys baking, but we're going to gain forty pounds this season alone if we don't slow down."

John smiled kindly as he turned away from the stove, where he had poured Lauri a cup of coffee from a blue enamel pot.

"I'll be able to eat on that for days. Thank you again, although the visit itself would have been enough."

"We've missed seeing you, too. Since Drake—" She cut off what she was about to say. *Since Drake left, we haven't felt like doing much of anything.* She concentrated on blowing on her coffee to cool it.

"Lauri, how do you feel about his going back?" The question was asked quietly, but Lauri couldn't ignore it. She glanced up at John as he joined them at the table with a mug of coffee in his giant hand.

"He—I—" Lauri choked on the words and tried to hide her emotion by reaching over to Jennifer and smoothing back the curls dangerously close to the chocolate icing that encircled her rosebud mouth. She looked up at her teacher with Drake's eyes—green, black-fringed. They were poignant reminders of him, and she felt the tears escape her eyelids and roll down her cheeks.

"Do you want to talk about it?" John asked. He

touched her hand, which rested listlessly on the checked tablecloth. His eyes were dark and warm and confidence-inspiring. She began to talk, and the whole story poured out.

John didn't interrupt her. He made no comment when she had to stop and blow her nose or choke back a fresh wave of tears. Jennifer, exhibiting a tenderness and understanding far beyond her years, came around to Lauri's side of the table and climbed into her lap. She rested her head against Lauri's chest and patted her shoulder comfortingly.

"We're not really married," she said hoarsely. "The ceremony was real enough, but the vows were false. They meant nothing to Drake."

"But they did to you?" John asked perceptively.

Lauri tried to answer but couldn't. She only looked up at him and nodded miserably. "I love him, John. I knew from the first time I saw him that I was going to love him, and I fought it. I fought it when I knew that I could never mean more to him than a warm body in bed." She felt no self-consciousness at this admission. John would never condemn anyone for loving. "In all fairness he warned me that he loved his wife and that he wouldn't get involved with anyone on a permanent basis."

She sniffed into the Kleenex, now soggy and shredded. Jennifer looked up at her with such concern that Lauri rubbed her back and smiled encouragingly. The child shouldn't see her this upset; Lauri was her only anchor.

It must truly shake the child's world to see her teacher/
mother in such a state of devastation.

"I think you've misjudged Drake, Lauri," John said.
"Don't be too sure that you're only a 'warm body in
bed' to him. He's left you with the responsibility of
virtually rearing his child for him. It's impossible for
him to have her with him all the time. It would be
difficult for any single male to rear a young child."

"I'm paid to do that, John. He could have hired someone else just as easily."

"Probably much more easily. But he didn't. In spite
of the fact that a beautiful woman living in any man's
house causes incalculable problems, he chose you."

"No, I was chosen for him. I came highly recom-
mended."

"All right," he sighed resignedly. "I'm not going to
argue that with you all day. There's something else."
His voice had changed considerably, and the different
quality she heard in it made her look up at him. "I've
seen Drake with you. I've seen the look in his eyes
when they light on you."

"What you're seeing is lust. There's an explosive
chemistry between us. I know he . . . wants me."

"No, Lauri. I've been guilty of lust," he laughed
deeply. "No, there's a distinct difference. Don't you
recognize love when you see it?" His smile was sad,
and his eyes conveyed more than one meaning to his
words. She parted her lips, intending to speak, but she
couldn't. There was nothing for her to say. John knew

it, for he continued hastily, "And I've never seen a man so jealous as Drake was that day I came to your house."

"He was jealous of Jennifer's affection for you," Lauri said. "He thought it highly improper that you and I were seeing each other." She laughed bitterly. "In the light of what Drake had in mind for me, his reaction to our one date a week with Jennifer serving as chaperon is funny. If it weren't so sad."

"This wife of his, she died three years ago?"

"Yes. Doctor Norwood told me that she died when Jennifer was only a few months old. That was the only fact I had, and Drake hasn't enlightened me further. His wife is off limits as far as conversation goes."

"Hmm." John said. "It's strange that a man of Drake's intelligence and self-confidence should continue to grieve for so long."

Lauri sighed deeply. "I can't understand it either, John. But it's sincere. There's no doubt in my mind about that."

She and Jennifer left a short while later. Her tears had provided a means to vent some of her depression, and she felt restored when she left John's house.

At the door he placed a heavy arm around her shoulders. "Lauri, if there's ever anything I can do, please don't hesitate to call me. I know what it is to hurt inside, and sometimes it helps to share it."

John, sometime in his life, had suffered unbearable grief. Intuitively Lauri knew that. Was that why he didn't censure other people? Was that why he was so understanding? Did he realize that a vicious action was usually the result of a wounded spirit?

Three weeks after their visit with John, the first blizzard of the season struck with full force. Though the days were monotonous, Lauri was more at peace with herself and her tenuous situation. She tried different methods of teaching Jennifer to speak and was rewarded when the child began to make noticeable progress.

On the afternoon of the blizzard the wind howled forebodingly while they sat in front of the mirror in the classroom trying to perfect thc sound of the letter *p*. Lauri held a cotton ball on her hand and demonstrated how it flew off when she made the sound properly. Jennifer imitated her actions and beamed with pride when she was able to produce the sound.

Lauri left her to practice with the cotton ball and went into the living room to investigate a noise she had heard outside. When she reached the wide windows, she peered out into the swirling snow through the heavy drapes. Her heart lurched at the sight of Drake climbing out of a four-wheel-drive vehicle and ducking his head to protect it from the wind as he rushed up the slippery steps to the porch.

He had raised his hand to knock, but Lauri rushed to the door and swung it open to let him inside. He shook the top of his head, which was dusted with snow, and folded down the collar of his shearling coat before turning to look at her.

"Lauri," he said.

She tried to say his name, but succeeded only in mouthing it.

"How are you?" he asked.

"F-fine," she stammered. Then she shook her head slightly, trying to clear it and said more firmly, "I'm— we're fine. Everything's fine." She wouldn't ask him what he was doing here. They had played that scene before.

"Where's Jennifer?" he asked.

"She's in the classroom. We've altered our schedule somewhat since you . . ." She trailed off. "It's more convenient this way," she explained lamely.

He didn't comment, only turned toward the classroom and walked through the door. Before she reached it, Lauri heard Jennifer's delighted squeal.

Drake was standing in the middle of the room with Jennifer in his arms. The child had her arms wrapped around his neck and her legs, as far as they would reach, around his chest. His hands were holding her under her bottom. Bunny, who had rarely been out of her hands since Drake left, lay forsaken beside her chair.

She leaned back and looked into her father's face. "Jen-fa, Jen-fa," she said, patting her chest with her hand. "Dau-dy. Dau-dy," she said, hugging him again.

"Oh, sweetheart, that's wonderful," he said, but she couldn't hear his praise. She only read it in his eyes. He looked toward Lauri, who still stood in the door, and grinned at her widely. "That's great, Lauri. She's doing well, isn't she?" He was the anxious parent who had sat across the table from her in the Russian Tea Room, and she said reassuringly, "Yes, Drake. She's doing very well."

He managed to free a hand long enough to extract two packages of gum from his pocket. Jennifer pounced on them greedily and he obliged her by opening one. It was evident that classes for the day were over.

There were a million questions reeling through Lauri's head, but she stifled the impulse to ask them. She would find out soon enough why he had shown up on the worst day of the year. The only thing she did ask was, "Would you like some cocoa or coffee? You must be freezing."

"Yes, please. I'm going to stop in the little boys' room and then I'll meet you in the kitchen."

Her hands trembled as she prepared the cocoa, which Drake had said he preferred. She took some of the cookies she and Jennifer had baked from the freezer and popped them into the microwave oven. The unmistakable aroma of fresh-baked cookies filled the kitchen.

"If I didn't know better, I'd think you were expecting me," Drake said, coming into the room and brushing back tousled hair with his fingers. The tight jeans rode low on his hips, and the light blue cable-knit sweater made his eyes glow green. Lauri swallowed hard. He was so blatantly sexy. Memories, explicit and vivid, crowded her mind. She forced her eyes away from him.

"Jennifer and I have been baking quite a bit. A few weeks ago, we baked John a chocolate cake." The spiteful gibe was intended to wound, and she knew it wasn't worthy of her.

If he were going to comment, he was prevented from doing so when Jennifer ran into the room, demanding to sit in Drake's lap while he sipped his cocoa. They communicated in sign for a few minutes, and Lauri was glad to see that he hadn't let his skills slip. If anything, he seemed more proficient.

"Well," he drawled, and leaned back in his chair after he had finished his cocoa and Jennifer had become interested in coloring a picture, "we have laid Doctor Glen Hambrick to rest."

"What!" Lauri exclaimed in astonishment. "What do you mean?"

"I mean," he said with a smile, "that he never recovered from the clout on the head he received in the park, remember?" At her nod he continued. "He died in his sleep without ever regaining consciousness. Poor chap," Drake said with exaggerated sympathy.

"What are you going to do, Drake?" Lauri had forgotten her earlier determination not to ask him any questions.

"Dau-dy." Jennifer distracted his attention to critique her drawing. When he had heaped the proper amount of praise on it, he turned back to Lauri who was impatiently waiting to hear his plans.

"There is a television movie coming up that I want

to do. A good production company is filming it. I heard about it through the grapevine and hopped on my agent to get off his duff and land me the part. I flew out to Hollywood and did a screen test. They like me. It's looking good." He looked away shyly. "It's about an autistic child who is deaf. They need someone who knows sign to play his father."

"Oh, Drake, that's marvelous," she said warmly and meant it.

"Are you familiar with the play on Broadway *Children of a Lesser God*? It's about the deaf and has received all sorts of awards."

"Yes, of course. I've seen it."

"Well, the guy who produced that is working with a playwright on another script that's similar. He's looking for a bright new director who wouldn't be afraid of taking on a challenge like that. I had lunch with him the other day."

"Drake, I'm so excited for you."

"Don't be. There are a million variables. Everything could go wrong." His face was serious then broke into that famous, heart-melting, dimpled smile. "But it's damn hard not to be excited, isn't it?"

"I hope everything works out the way you want it to. You won't miss Doctor Hambrick?"

"Maybe I'll suffer some withdrawal pains, but I don't think they'll last. The best thing is that I'll be able to spend more time with Jennifer. I may have to move from coast to coast for a while, and the hours won't improve much, but in between jobs we can take vacations just like other families." He reached over to pat his daughter's head and didn't see Lauri's shattered look.

She rose abruptly from the table and busied herself in getting a casserole—one of their projects on a rainy day—out of the freezer and putting it in the oven for dinner.

Drake chatted on. "It may be tough for a while. I'll have to watch the budget, something I haven't had to do the last several years. But I've managed to save enough to live on if times get hard." He laughed. "Believe it or not, my agent is ecstatic. He says clients are clamoring for my face to endorse everything from toothpaste to panty hose. You work one day and make a lot of money if it's a national commercial. I haven't bothered with them before, but I'll take advantage of my visibility now."

She washed lettuce under the faucet. "I'm sure you'll be a success, Drake. At whatever you do."

She was glad when he offered to take Jennifer out of the way while she finished preparing dinner. As soon as they had left the room, she slumped against the countertop and covered her face with her hands.

He had all but told her she was fired. Not only had he not mentioned their phony marriage and their affair, but he had intimated that he would be able to spend more time with Jennifer, making Lauri superfluous. He was paying her more than a generous salary. Money wouldn't be in as great a supply as it had been. He was going to have to cut corners, she would no doubt be one of them.

There would be no trouble in her finding another job. A teacher of the deaf was always in demand, but there would be no joy in accepting another position. She would constantly be worrying about the pupil she had come to look upon as a daughter.

You knew there was a danger in getting too close, too involved, Lauri, she chided herself. Now you'll pay dearly for doing just that.

One thought consoled her. Jennifer was too young to remember her for long. She would miss Lauri initially, but she would soon recover and forget. Lauri told herself that the thought was comforting. Why then was it so painful to contemplate?

"Lauri?" She jumped when Drake said her name from the doorway of the kitchen. Composing her face, she turned to him. "Yes?"

"Are those boxes with Susan's things in them still upstairs in that closet?"

Her hands were clenched behind her back, and she could feel the nails biting into her palms. A lump rose in her throat, yet she managed to answer calmly enough, "Yes. I haven't touched them."

"Okay" was all he said as he slapped the doorjamb and walked away.

It took several moments for her to recover. How could

he ask her something like that and not show any regard for her feelings? Did he think she had given herself to him lightly? Were those nights in his bed to be forgotten as if they had never happened?

Did he think she could forget the touch of his accomplished hands and mouth? She recalled the whispered words of love he had used while coaching her in ways to please him. He had murmured encouragement and praise each time he brought her back from that region where everything gave off dazzling light. Again and again, and in ways previously unknown, he had taken her there. But he was always waiting on the other side to hold her, stroke her, and cherish her.

At dinnertime he chatted amiably, relishing the home-cooked meal that, he said, was his first since returning to New York. He told her all the gossip about town: who was seen with whom in which posh disco. She responded only when required to. When he asked about Betty and her family, she related one anecdote about Sam and a can of paint at which he howled with laughter. Jennifer was able to follow the signs and added her own description of the mishap. She joined Drake's laughter.

After the meal Drake began helping with the dishes, but Lauri shooed him away. "You need to spend some time with Jennifer," she said.

"Okay. I wanted to tell her something important anyway," he said as he followed Lauri's suggestion and left the kitchen to find his daughter.

The dishes were done, and Lauri could think of nothing else with which to occupy herself. She had deliberately dragged out the preparations of the meal and the cleaning up, but now she had no choice but to spend some time with Drake.

Lord, give me strength, she prayed as she went into the living room. How could she stand to be with him and not be a part of him? Could she be within touching distance and not touch? Since he had walked in, shaking the snow from his coat, she had longed to go to him and thrill again to his embrace. That was out of the question. More than likely, in a matter of days, she would exit his life forever.

She was checking the latch at the front door to make sure it was bolted when she heard Drake's voice coming from the classroom. It reached her even over the roar of the wind and the *ping* of sleet against the windows.

"Mom-my," Drake said distinctly and with stress on the syllables. "Feel here, Jennifer," she heard him say. "Put your fingers here on my throat. Mom-my. Mom-my. See? Can you do it?"

"Mau-my," Lauri heard Jennifer say with an effort.

"Yes!" she heard Drake say as he patted the child on the back "That's close," he said. "Here's what it looks like written. M-O-M-M-Y. Mom-my. Try it again," he urged.

Lauri covered her mouth to stifle the cry of anguish that burst from her throat. The pictures! He had asked if Susan's things were still upstairs. He must have got some of the things to help explain to Jennifer her relationship to the woman in the photographs.

"I can't bear it," Lauri gasped, and ran upstairs. The moment she opened the bedroom door, she saw that the closet doors containing the boxes were open. He had looked through them and taken out what he wanted to show his daughter.

Oh, God, Lauri sobbed. He still loves her. He always will. Subconsciously she had been entertaining the hope that his return meant he had reconsidered their relationship. Perhaps he wanted their fake marriage to be made legally binding. Now she knew better.

She also knew what she had to do.

Without thinking further, she took a suitcase from underneath the bed and began to pack. She took only what was necessary. She would ask Betty to send the rest of her things to her later. Right now she didn't even have an address.

When she was finished, she snapped the suitcase shut and slid it once again under the bed. She didn't want to alert Drake to her plans.

Lauri Parrish was a fighter. Surrendering to anything was a loathsome offense to her character. Only once before in her lifetime had she had been forced to retreat—when her marriage had reached a point where remedy was impossible.

She was a fighter, but when defeat was inevitable, when victory was beyond her grasp, she knew how to surrender gracefully no matter how much it hurt her pride. She accepted the hopelessness of Drake's ever returning her love. She was leaving—now. While she still retained a modicum of dignity.

She was waving the white flag.

Chapter Fourteen

❦

I t seemed to take forever to get Jennifer ready for bed. She was excited over Drake's presence in the house and pulled stunts that Lauri would never have countenanced at any other time.

Finally she was bathed, kissed, and tucked in. When she said the prayer Lauri had taught her in sign language, Lauri blinked back stinging tears. She knelt down and hugged the child closer, reveling in her clean, fresh smell and the petal softness of her skin. *I love you, Jennifer*, she signed before she fled the room, leaving Drake to turn out the light.

She went into the master bedroom and shut the door, but within seconds, Drake was knocking on it. "Yes?"

"Room service," he said cheekily before opening the door himself. "Why don't you come down and drink a glass of wine with me in front of the fireplace. It's a perfect night for it." His sly insinuation was that it was a perfect night for other things as well.

His words filled her with rage, and it was a taxing effort to contain it. He sill thought that he could use her at his convenience. Well, he'd soon know that she was made of finer stuff than that!

"I have a headache," she said tritely. "I think it was caused by the wind blowing all day or something. Anyway, I don't feel well. I think I'll go to bed. What I need more than a glass of wine is a good night's sleep."

"The lady doth protest too much methinks."

"I'm sorry, Drake. I just don't feel like going downstairs again," she said curtly.

He stared at her a moment then said, "All right. I'll see you in the morning."

She had listened to the muffled sounds of the television set as she paced in her room. Finally it was turned off, and she heard Drake go into the room adjoining the kitchen. Water splashed in the bathroom as he got ready for bed.

At last the house was quiet. Lauri crept to the top of the stairs and listened. No lights were on. Returning to her room, she waited another twenty minutes before she slipped on her coat and hood, retrieved her suitcase from beneath the bed, and crept stealthily down the stairs.

The wind had died down, but it was still snowing hard when Lauri stepped out onto the front porch. After quietly putting down her suitcase, she pulled the door closed behind her. Cautiously she crept down the icy steps and half slid, half walked to the parked Mercedes.

The door to the car was frozen shut. After several frustrated attempts to open it with one hand, she had to place her shoulder bag and suitcase on the snow and pull with both hands before the door swung open, nearly knocking her down.

She stowed her bags in the backseat and slid behind the wheel. Through her leather gloves, she could feel that the steering wheel was ice cold, and she shivered under her heavy coat. What if the car wouldn't start?

She pumped the accelerator several times, then tried the ignition. The engine made a grating sound, chugged, and stopped.

"Damn!" she muttered under her breath as she tried again. When she was about to give up, the engine jumped to life and the purr of the motor was a blessed sound. All the time she was trying to start the car, she kept a nervous eye on the front door, fearful that Drake would hear the motor. Apparently the whistling wind muffled any other sound. With one final, regretful look toward the house, she engaged the gears, and the wheels of the car fought for traction on the slippery ground.

Her thoughts had been so jumbled that she hadn't really given any thought to driving during a blizzard. She was accustomed to driving on snowy streets in Nebraska. But these mountains in New Mexico were different from the flat plains of her home state.

Panic engulfed her as the wheels lost their traction

and swerved to one side of the lane. She managed to right the car's course, but she gnawed her bottom lip nervously. Taking a firmer grip on the steering wheel, she was determined not to go back. Drake had driven from Albuquerque in this storm. If he had made the trip, so could she. If she waited until morning, everything would be frozen even harder.

It took her almost ten minutes to negotiate the lane that led to the house. When she reached the bottom of the hill where the lane intersected with the road going into the village proper, she applied the brakes, but the car refused to stop. Thinking she could ease out into the street without coming to a complete stop, she turned the steering wheel no more than a fraction of an inch.

But it was sufficient.

Before she could regain control, the car was lost to her and under its own guidance. It careened crazily, its rear wheels fishtailing first to one side of the lane, then the other. Instinctively Lauri slammed on the brakes. The wheels locked, and the rear of the car plunged down into the soft bank of snow in the ditch. She lay reclined in the seat as if she were in a dental chair. She was unhurt. There couldn't have been much damage to the car, for its descent into the ditch had been easy and she had heard no crunching of metal. It was, however, hopelessly sunk in the deep snow. She cut the engine.

Before she had a chance to ponder her dilemma, the door on the driver's side was ripped open, and she stifled a scream before she saw Drake's face. It didn't resemble his usual physiognomy, but instead was contorted with anger.

"Are you hurt?" he barked.

She shook her head dumbly, not knowing whether to be glad she had survived the accident or not. She was more afraid of Drake now than she was of the possibility of an automobile crash.

He grabbed her by the upper arm and dragged her from behind the wheel. When she resisted and tried to reach for her bags in the backseat he yelled, "Leave them." He had put on his shearling coat, but had left it unbuttoned, and it flapped around him as he struggled up the side of the ditch in the knee-deep snow. The blowing snow and Stygian darkness hindered their progress even more. He pulled her along behind him, caring little that the snow was midthigh on her.

She called out to him once when she thought her ankle was going to snap in the heel of her boot, but he didn't hear her. Or he was ignoring her.

When at last they had climbed out of the ditch, she was grateful for the chance to rest, but Drake had other ideas. Taking a firmer grip on her arm, he began to march up the lane, stumbling, sliding, and cursing with each step. She never remembered seeing him this angry. His head was bare, yet he seemed impervious to the bitter cold wind and the snow that was capping his windblown hair.

She was soon exhausted and lagged behind. He jerked her upright and hissed close to her ear, "If you don't get your ass in gear, my footprints are going to be covered up with more snow. Then we'll be lost out here. Is that what you want?" He shook her slightly and she looked up at him fearfully. She shook her head no, and they continued on their way up the hill.

She slipped on the steps leading to the front porch and fell forward, catching herself with her hands. Drake placed his hands under her arms and hauled her up without ceremony or gentleness. He shoved the front door open with his shoulder and pushed her inside.

Her feet were frozen and felt like wooden blocks as she tramped toward the stairs. Her intention was to escape Drake. He must have gleaned that, for he was right behind her, and, gripping her wrist in a fist made of iron, pulled her toward the fireplace.

"Don't you dare move," he ordered in a menacing voice. He knelt down and stirred the glowing coals with a poker before placing more logs on the grate. When they had ignited to his satisfaction, he turned to Lauri.

Had she not been chilled to the bone and shivering already, his look would have frozen her blood. The green eyes flashed with fury. His jaw was hard and indomitable.

She flinched when he raised his arms. Instead of striking her as she expected, he clenched her shoulders and drew her closer to him until she had to tilt her head back painfully on her neck to see him.

"If you ever pull another stunt like that, I'll blister your butt. Do you hear me?" He shook her again, and her head wobbled uselessly. "What were you trying to prove?" he demanded. "Huh?" he added when she didn't answer him.

The fire was gradually warming her and with the thaw came the anger. By what right did he cross-examine her? She was a free agent. She could leave if she wanted to, and without any explanation to him.

She yanked herself out of his grasp and backed away from him, her anger matching his. They were now squared off like boxers, each assessing the opponent's strength.

"If it's your car you're worried about, I left you a note upstairs informing you that it would be left in the airport parking lot to be picked up at your convenience." Her chin inclined slightly with belligerence.

"I wasn't worried about a goddamn car!" he roared. "Did you leave Jennifer a note, too, explaining your sneaking away? I'm sure she would have wondered where you were," he sneered.

That momentarily set her back and she mumbled something unintelligible.

"I didn't catch that," he said, crossing his arms over his chest in an arrogant stance that infuriated her.

"I *said*," she emphasized, "that I would leave the explanations to you."

"And what would I tell her?"

The fiery glow of her hair matched the anger building within her. It was her only defense against his insolence. "Tell her that I hold myself in higher esteem than to be the part-time mistress of an actor who expects every woman to grovel before him. Tell her that as much as I love her and care about her future, I couldn't stay and be insulted and degraded by a meaningless, shabby affair. I was being paid to teach her, not to provide bedroom services to her father."

Her breasts were heaving with agitation, and her body was pulled as taut as a violin string. "I'm leaving here if I have to walk! I don't care if I ever see you again, Drake Sloan." She whirled away from him.

"No," he said with a rasping hoarseness.

Lauri was so startled by the raw emotion in his voice that she halted. Curious about his swift change of mood, she faced him again. His eyes, which had been full of anger only moments before, now looked bleak, desperate, and pleading.

"I won't let you leave me. Lauri. Say you won't." While she watched with incredulity, he dropped to his knees and wrapped his arms around her waist. His face was pressed against her softness and he nuzzled her gently. "I swore I'd never love another woman. But I do. God help me, I do. I won't let you leave," he repeated.

Her hands went of their own accord to the top of his head, and she brushed the remaining drops of moisture from the silver-tinted strands. Pushing away from him, she sank to her knees to face him.

"Drake? What are you saying?" She searched his face for signs of deceit. Was he role-playing? Was this the tender, tragic scene at the end of the play when the future of the lovers hangs in the balance? No. The pain and longing and despair she saw on his face were genuine. He wasn't acting.

He brushed away the snow-dampened tendrils of auburn hair beside her cheek and said softly, "You thought I waltzed in here today and expected to pick up where we left off, right?" She nodded. "And you thought that when I invited you to come down here and share a glass of wine with me that I was setting the big seduction scene, right?" She nodded, "Well, I was," he confessed abashedly. "But first I was going to ask you to make our marriage a real one. Or rather a *legal* one. I've always felt that the one your father performed was real."

"Drake," she whispered, "why didn't you tell me any of this before?"

"*Why?*" he scoffed. "Would you have believed me? You're always so defensive, looking for ulterior motives, never trusting an honest emotion when you see it." He leaned forward and pressed his lips against her forehead.

"I understand you better than you understand yourself, Lauri Parrish Rivington," he said. "I told you on our second meeting that your face was too expressive for your own good." He outlined the bones of her face with loving, adoring fingers.

"Paul must have been a real bastard. From what little you've told me, I think I can fill in the gaps and see what kind of life you had with him. He was moody and temperamental, and you felt like you were walking on eggshells all the time in order not to damage his fragile self-image. Am I right?"

"Yes," she said. How had he known all that?

"Well, I can be as moody and temperamental as the next person. In fact, I can be as mean as hell. But you've certainly never hesitated to show me that fierce temper of yours when I get too far out of line. You knew, whether your mind thought on it consciously or not, that I'm not like Paul. I'm tougher. I'm not as fragile. I won't ever lean on a crutch like alcohol to keep from facing adversity.

"Living with anybody who is constantly in the public eye is tough. I realize that. But no matter what people say or what you read about me, don't believe it unless I say it's true. If things ever get too hard to handle, I'd get out and do something else. To me, acting is a profession, not a passion. You and Jennifer would always come first."

He drew a deep breath. "Now, if you can put up with a tiny bit of artistic temperament, I can put up with your fiery temper."

"Fiery temper!" she cried with an instant display of the subject. She had fallen for his trick, and he laughed. Embarrassed, she joined his laughter, then collapsed against him and said, "No, you're nothing like Paul. And I trust you now." Her heart was pounding with joy, but she had to clear away all the doubts and . . . ghosts.

"Drake, what about Susan?"

"Susan?" he asked, raising his head and looking down at her. "I thought you might ask me about her." He sighed.

Oh, God, no! Lauri screamed inside. "You still love her, don't you?" she asked, surprised at her own temerity.

He stared at her in shock. "Is *that* what you thought?"

She nodded "The first time you kissed me, you told me you loved your wife."

"In the past tense, yes. I did. When we first met, I loved her deeply. We had fun together. Our sex life was more than satisfactory."

Lauri was suffocated with jealousy, and it must have showed. The corners of Drake's lips lifted in a grin before they relaxed and became serious again.

"She was beautiful and talented. But she didn't have a generous spirit; she had no soul. As much as I hate to admit it, she was spoiled, selfish, and shallow. Her ambition nearly drove me to distraction, because it included me as well as her." As he talked he shrugged out of his coat and helped Lauri with hers.

"She virtually forced me to take that soap opera job I didn't want. She wasn't willing to sacrifice and let me continue studying. She wanted to be married to a celebrity, as if that were worth anything," he said bitterly. "But she gloried in that celebrity life—and in dance. When she got pregnant, I thought she was going to castrate me. She hadn't wanted to take birth control pills because they made her gain weight, but it was all *my* fault when she got pregnant."

They were leaning against the hearth, his arm supporting her. He held her hand and traced each vein and bone with his finger. "Such lovely hands," he murmured and brought one to his mouth, kissing the palm before continuing his story.

"I was almost afraid that she'd have an abortion, but after nine months of griping temper tantrums and incessant bitching, she delivered Jennifer, and I was thrilled."

He paused again and stood up, facing the fire. The flickering shadows etched the features of his face sharply. "Jennifer was six months old when we discovered she was deaf. Can you imagine the mental anguish, Lauri? The soul-searching? Was I being punished for some secret sin? Stealing apples when I was ten years old? I realize how ridiculous that self-incrimination was now, but that was my first reaction. But it was nothing compared to Susan's. As if my own guilt weren't enough, Susan blamed me too. 'I didn't want the kid in the first place,' she'd scream at me. You see, Jennifer didn't meet Susan's standard, which was perfection. Susan's dancing had to be perfect; she wanted a perfect husband. She couldn't cope with having a less than perfect child."

He was silent a long while as he stirred the logs with the toe of his boot, pushing them closer to the coals. "One day I came home late from the studio. I could hear Jennifer crying in her room. When I went in there, I nearly retched. She was lying in her own waste. She was cold and hungry. I was furious with Susan and stormed through the apartment looking for her. She . . . she—"

He couldn't continue, and Lauri's heart filled with pity when he covered his face with both hands. She knew what was coming. She didn't speak or go to him. He would always have to suffer this particular hell alone. No one else could ever share it. She had been spared finding Paul's body, but could empathize with Drake's horrifying recollection.

"She was in the bathtub with both wrists slashed. It was obvious that she had been dead for some time." After a long interval of silence he came back to her side and sat down on the rug, putting his arms around her and holding her against him.

"I never forgave her. I let her parents arrange the funeral, which I refused to attend. Her family made it unequivocably clear that they never wanted to have anything to do with me or Jennifer again. We had robbed them of their treasure, their princess. Lauri" —he pushed her away from him so he could look into her eyes— "I swore that I would never love anyone again. I had loved Susan, and when I needed her the most, when we needed the full support and love from each other, she deserted me. But I fell in love with you. That's why you can't leave me now. I need you, don't you see?" He kissed her in desperation. His lips didn't need to demand a response. She was only too willing to let him know how much she loved him.

When at last they pulled apart he said, "I went to New York to get things settled career-wise, but also to exorcise her ghost and visit her grave. I had never even been there. I can't tell you the hatred and bitterness I harbored against her. I realize now that she couldn't help being what she was any more than any of us can. Until I learned what it was to love, I couldn't forgive. Now I know: a beautiful little redhead taught me. I began to realize what it was all about that day Jennifer made the mess with your makeup. You were justifiably mad and you punished her, but you also forgave her. She never doubted your love. I had to go back and forgive Susan before I could offer you my love. I wanted it to be untarnished."

Another deep kiss followed, then she said, "You asked about the boxes in the closet this afternoon. I thought you were going to show the pictures of Susan to Jennifer. I heard you teaching her to say *Mommy*."

"So that's what set you off!" He threw back his head and laughed. "I asked for the boxes because now I can stand to sort through them. Before, I hated touching anything that belonged to her. I chose what I wanted to save for Jennifer. One day, when she's old enough to understand, we'll have to tell her about her mother."

He placed a hand under her chin and raised it so she had to look at him "And I was teaching Jennifer to say *Mommy* as a surprise for you. That's what I want her to call you from now on. As soon as we're legally married, that's what you'll be."

"Drake—" she started to say before his mouth closed over hers.

"Are you getting warmer?" Lauri cooed. Then: "Drake—" with a gasp. With inquisitive hands he was inspecting her body under the foamy bubbles in the deep bathtub. Despite her protest he wasn't deterred. He touched her in a way that made her neck arch as a long sigh escaped her parted lips. She glanced at their reflection in the mirrors opposite the bathtub and, though she had lit the room with only candlelight, their images were clear.

"When did you think up this decadent activity?" he asked.

"The first time I walked in this bathroom," she giggled. "I saw us together in here like this. I wanted to cover Jennifer's eyes before I realized the mirage existed only in my wicked imagination. Of course," she added thoughtfully, "I think she may have inherited your immodesty."

"Am I so immodest?"

"You told me that since you toured with *Hair*, you had absolutely no modesty."

"Did I say that?" he asked in surprise. "I lied. I've never been in *Hair*. I just needed a guaranteed way to get into that bed with you naked."

"Oh, you!" She splashed water in his face, but licked it away leisurely. As she went about that enticing occupation, his fingers teased her unmercifully. He asked huskily, "Do you know when I first fell in love with you?"

"Drake," she sighed as he found an arousing spot. "No, when?" she asked hastily, afraid she would soon be unable to breathe.

"When we were in the Russian Tea Room and you were honest with me about Jennifer and what I could expect of her." He grinned lewdly. "Though I was attracted to that little firebrand who spurned Drake Sloan, not giving a damn if he were a superstar or not. You looked gorgeous that day. I stripped off every garment piece by piece in my mind. But the reality far surpassed the fantasy." His hands lent credence to his words.

"When did you know that you loved me?" he asked after a kiss in which his tongue gathered the sweetness of her mouth and took it into himself.

"Have I ever said that I love you?" she asked impishly.

His reaction startled her. He rolled over on her, not caring that water sloshed over the side of the tub. "Do you? Do you, Lauri?"

With fingers dripping foamy water, she signed, *I love you with all my heart.* She spoke with an eloquent silence more expressive than voiced language. Her silken thighs moved sensuously along his under the warm water, conveying a message all their own. His eyes dropped to her breasts that bobbed in the water, tempting him beyond endurance.

His mouth closed over each pink bud, teasing it with

teeth and tongue before suckling it. His hips fit more snugly into the welcoming hollows of her.

Sipping at her wet skin, he said, "The roads will be impassable for the next few days. Until we can get into Albuquerque or Santa Fe to get legally married, will you consent to live in sin?"

Her tongue teased his chest, his chin, his mustache, even as her hands clasped the backs of his thighs and applied suppliant pressure until she could feel him hard and eager against her.

"What would you do if I said no?" she asked playfully.

"I'd drown you," he growled, lowering his head once again.

"Yes, drown me, Drake," she said, arching against him. "With your love."